Don't Sneeze at the Wedding

For Amy, my shining star—P.M.

To the girls in my life: Caro, Renata, Miranda,
Sabina, Marina, Arantxa, Ximena—M.A.

KAR-BEN PUBLISHING, INC.
A division of Lerner Publishing Group, Inc.
241 First Avenue North
Minneapolis, MN 55401 U.S.A.
1-800-4-Karben

Website address: www.karben.com

Library of Congress Cataloging-in-Publication Data

Mayer, Pamela.
    Don't sneeze at the wedding / by Pamela Mayer ; illustrated by Martha Avilés.
        p.   cm.
    Summary: "A young flower girl with a cold gets advice on how to avoid sneezing during
her aunt's wedding ceremony."—Provided by publisher.
    ISBN: 978-1-4677-0428-1 (lib. bdg : alk. paper)
    ISBN: 978-1-4677-1641-3 (eBook)
    [1. Sneezing—Fiction. 2. Weddings—Fiction. 3. Jews—Fiction.] I. Avilés Junco, Martha, ill.
II. Title. III. Title: Do not sneeze at the wedding.
PZ7.M463Don 2013
[E]—dc23   2012029188

Manufactured in the United States of America
1 - PC - 7/15/13

Don't Sneeze at the Wedding

Pamela Mayer

Illustrated by

Martha Avilés

KAR-BEN
PUBLISHING

On the morning of Aunt Rachel's wedding I woke up and... **Ah-Choo!**

Mommy felt my forehead for fever.

Daddy peered at my throat.

"I'm fine," I said, "just sneezy." **Ah-Choo!**

"Please don't sneeze at the wedding!" my parents said together.

"If you feel a sneeze coming, press your upper lip with your finger, like this." Daddy showed me.

I put my finger on my lip and repeated, "Press lip, don't sneeze."

I hurried through breakfast, because I couldn't wait
to put on my flower girl dress. I love, love, love it.
It's pale pink, with tiny buttons and a sash, and I
have pink shoes to match.

When we got to the Temple, Grandma met us at the door.

"Anna, you look so gorgeous," she said with a hug.

"Thank you," I said, twirling so my dress flared out. *Ah-Choo!*

"Oh dear," Grandma said. "Please don't sneeze at the wedding!"

She handed me a tissue. "If you think you are going to sneeze, wiggle your earlobe. That will stop it."

"Okay," I said. "Press lip, wiggle earlobe, don't sneeze."

We went to the special room where Aunt Rachel and her bridesmaids were getting dressed. Monsieur Phillippe was busily arranging their hair and applying make-up.

"Ah, our petite flower girl!" he exclaimed. "A little curl and perhaps some lip gloss, *oui*?"

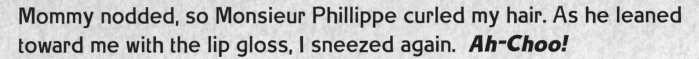

Mommy nodded, so Monsieur Phillippe curled my hair. As he leaned toward me with the lip gloss, I sneezed again. **Ah-Choo!**

"*Sacre bleu*," said Monsieur Phillippe. "Please don't sneeze at the wedding. If you feel a sneeze coming, *cherie*, just say 'pineapple.'"

"Press lip, wiggle earlobe, say 'pineapple,' don't sneeze." I reminded myself.

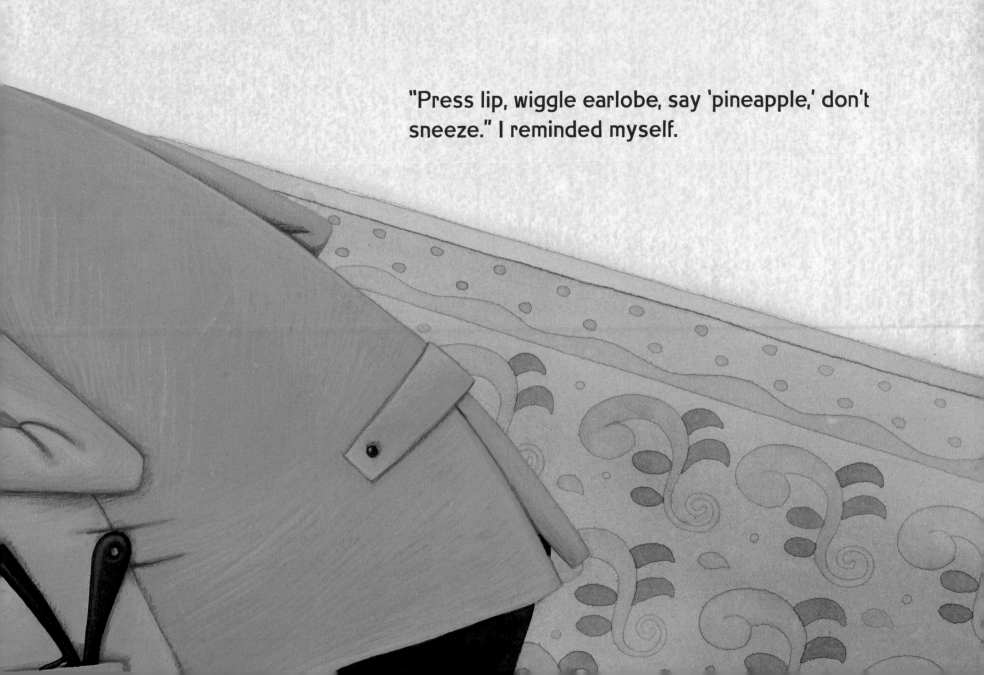

We heard a knock. "Betty's Flowers," a voice said. The florist came in, loaded down with boxes.

Aunt Rachel's bouquet was a cascade of flowers. I had a basket filled with rose petals, and a flowered wreath for my hair.

As Betty placed it on my head, I sneezed so loudly, my wreath nearly fell off. **Ah-Choo!**

"Golly gee, hon, please don't sneeze at the wedding," Betty said. "I've heard that if you tap your forehead between your eyes, you can stop a sneeze."

I sighed. Press lip, wiggle earlobe, say "pineapple," tap forehead, don't sneeze. So much to remember.

The door opened again. "Glenn's Photography. Let's get started with pictures of our lovely bride."

Soon it was my turn to pose with Aunt Rachel. Just as Glenn's assistant tilted my head, I looked into the camera, and...*Ah-Choo!*

"*Gesundheit*," Glenn said. "Just please don't sneeze at the wedding, little lady. A sure fire way to stop a sneeze is to pinch your nose."

Glenn demonstrated as I went over my growing list: Press lip, wiggle earlobe, say "pineapple," tap forehead, pinch nose, don't sneeze.

Then it was on to the rabbi's study to sign the ketubah.
I looked over Uncle Matt's shoulder, and . . . ***Ah-Choo!***

"Bless you!" Rabbi Bernstein said. "When I need to sneeze during a sermon, Anna, I hold my breath for a moment and that always stops it."

I sat down and thought over all of the stop sneezing suggestions.

Then it was time for the ceremony.

I didn't sneeze when I walked down the aisle.

I didn't sneeze when Aunt Rachel joined Uncle Matt under the chuppah.

I didn't sneeze when they shared a cup of wine.

I didn't sneeze when they exchanged rings, or when the rabbi sang the Seven Blessings.

But just as Rabbi Bernstein placed a wine glass wrapped in cloth next to Uncle Matt's foot, I felt a sneeze coming on.

Ah - ah

I pressed my finger to my lip.

I wiggled my ear lobe

and whispered "pineapple".

Uncle Matt raised his foot over the glass.

Ah - ah - ah

and held my breath.

I tapped my forehead between my eyes,

pinched my nose,

But as his heel came down, I just couldn't stop it.

At the sound of breaking glass, everyone shouted, **"Mazel Tov!"**
And it was so loud that it drowned out the sound of my sneeze.

Rabbi Bernstein winked at me and whispered, "*Gezundheit*, Anna. To your health."

Aunt Rachel and Uncle Matt kissed. Then they walked down the aisle together.

I sneezed at the wedding, after all, but only the rabbi heard!

About Jewish Weddings

A Jewish wedding takes place under a chuppah, a wedding canopy. A symbol of the home the new couple will create, it is open on four sides, like the tent of Abraham and Sarah, which was always open to guests.

The traditional ketubah is a marriage contract spelling out the groom's obligations to provide for his bride. Contemporary ketubot often contain the couple's individual hopes for their marriage.

The Seven Blessings, *sheva b'rachot*, thank God for the blessings of life and creation, and for the happiness of the bride and groom.

The breaking of the glass at the end of the ceremony has many meanings. Some say it is a reminder of the destruction of the Temple in Jerusalem. Others say that it tells us that even in times of great joy we should remember that the world is not yet a perfect place. Still others say it reminds us that relationships are fragile like glass and must be tended with care.

Guests all shout "Mazel Tov!" to wish the couple good luck.

ABOUT THE AUTHOR
Pamela Mayer was born and raised in San Francisco, California, and her family has lived there since the early 1900s. Writing children's stories is her favorite thing to do. When she's not writing, she works at the public library as a children's librarian. She's a fan of the San Francisco Giants baseball team, the San Francisco Ballet, and any and all circuses. She and her husband have two daughters and a very cute dog named Charlie.

ABOUT THE ILLUSTRATOR
Martha Avilés was born and raised in Mexico City. She has illustrated many children's books including *Say Hello, Lily*, *The Shabbat Princess*, and *Stones for Grandpa*.

W9-BLM-378

The Makeup
of a
Confident Woman

The Makeup
of a
Confident Woman

THE SCIENCE OF BEAUTY,

THE GIFT OF TIME,

AND THE POWER OF PUTTING

YOUR BEST FACE FORWARD

by Trish McEvoy

with Kristin Loberg

HarperCollins books may be purchased for educational, business,
or sales promotional use. For information, please email the
Special Markets Department at SPsales@harpercollins.com.

First Edition

Designed by Doug Turshen with Steve Turner

Library of Congress Cataloging-in-Publication Data has been applied for.

ISBN 978-0-06-249542-6

17 18 19 20 21   lsc   10 9 8 7 6 5 4 3 2 1

CONTENTS

To Ron, my greatest teacher and my greatest love.

XOX
TRISH

FOREWORD

I have had the great pleasure of knowing Trish McEvoy for decades and always enjoy our time together. We seem to be cut from similar cloth, worker bees who believe in dressing up, showing up, and never giving up. I deeply respect how Trish navigates life, taking pleasure in the joys of the moment even amidst the maelstrom. To me this is the mark and makeup of a confident woman, one who is prepared to handle life's highest stakes and smallest details with dignity and grace.

Trish has created success on her own terms—the most important terms of all—and I attribute how she has done so to the human values and tools to confidence she reveals in these pages. I have great affection for this woman who is not only a trailblazing makeup artist, innovator, and businesswoman but now, with her wonderful new book, an artisan of life who will help readers wring the most from their beauty and time.

—*Barbara Walters*

The Confidence Cure

A COUNTERINTUITIVE APPROACH TO RADIATING
CONFIDENCE FROM THE OUTSIDE IN

I have had the great privilege of helping women around the world with their beauty confidence for more than thirty years. Women like you who want to take on the day—whatever challenges may come—and exude a positive self-image, can-do attitude, and sense of calm. This is the beauty of the truly confident woman.

At its core, beauty is not just physical. It manifests in the way you present yourself, act, experience the world, and influence how others perceive you. This is why most confidence-building techniques teach us to start from the inside out, aiming to change our attitude and sense of self through cognitive exercises: hard, important, and necessary work for all of us.

But what if there were a way to jump-start that process of transformation in a matter of minutes? What if there was a shortcut to total beauty confidence? There is: By harnessing the connection between taking time for yourself to look and, in turn, feel your best, you can work *from the outside in*. And I'm going to give you a practical system for doing just that.

You've picked up this book for a reason. Somewhere deep down you know that there's a hidden power to makeup. And you know that when you are confident, anything is possible.

I've been teaching and talking about makeup's ability to empower for decades. Once you've experienced it, you will feel an immediate shift in your consciousness. That's right: your entire consciousness. And it will happen if you follow my program. Even if you're the type of woman who is perfectly fine without any makeup on, you can't deny the fact you feel like a better, up-leveled version of yourself with it on.

THE POWER OF BEAUTY CONFIDENCE

There is a strong correlation between confidence and how we show up in the world. Studies reveal that striking a commanding pose, whether you are in casual jeans or an evening gown, can change how you regard yourself, which, in turn, influences how you are regarded by others. Women know this instinctively. We also know that there's power in a face that's brightened, defined, and fine-tuned by makeup.

Nearly 70 percent of women globally think that being beautiful helps them get what they want out of life, and the same number believe that the relationship between happiness and beauty is directly proportional. In large surveys, a whopping 93 percent of women say they feel more confident overall when they believe they are presenting their best selves. It's no wonder that beauty rituals have been around since time immemorial. Whether it is makeup or adornment in ancient civilizations or modern day, making ourselves more beautiful is part of what makes us human.

Beyond the anecdotal evidence and hunches we have about the power of beauty, we also have science to prove it: Physically attractive people are more attractive in life. They earn more money, get promoted more readily, and have an advantage in any marketplace. Success, in fact, correlates just as closely with confidence as it does with competence. And the attractiveness that garners success has less to do with what attributes you were born with than what you make of them.

Beauty is confidence, and confidence is beautiful.

Cultivating the seeds to the beauty that transcends physicality is what this book is about, and it's easier than you think. The key is a simple but profound rethinking of your time in order to establish a few basic habits to look your best, which results in correspondingly dramatic changes in your lifestyle and perspective.

We live in a world so different from the one in which I started my makeup company decades ago. Women today are more time-starved, distracted by ongoing busy-ness, and routinely overwhelmed by responsibilities while pursuing monumental ambitions—education, degrees, careers, businesses, marriage, parenthood. Our lives have a lot of moving parts, yet at the end of the day we all want the same things. We want to feel beautiful, fearless, and in control of our lives. We want to be fulfilled by the work we do, and appreciated by others. All in all, we want to find our own special place in the world and love where we are in life. The good news is this system continues to work time and time again, no matter how complex our individual lives get and how the world changes around us. This system will be the constant in your life that enables you to achieve total beauty security, personal empowerment, and an understanding of the gift of time. As much as it can transform you, it can also *transport* you.

When you think about makeup, what comes to mind? Are you someone whose mother taught you the value of makeup or did you have to figure it out on your own? Does makeup intimidate you? Enthrall you? Perhaps you don't even think about it all that much, or you're a little ambivalent (but I don't believe you, because you're reading this book). Does it feel like a chore to put on, or are you like me, someone who absolutely adores it and treats it like a fundamental necessity? Maybe you are someone in between the extremes—you enjoy makeup and what it does for you but putting it on can seem like a tedious task on some days.

Most women I meet for the first time have tried to establish a beauty routine in the past, or are trying to upgrade their current one. They've navigated the cosmetics aisle on their own at their corner drugstore buying makeup that they'll use once and never again. They've watched YouTube videos of the latest makeup fads and failed in applying them to their own faces and lifestyles. And sometimes these attempts work for a little while. But eventually, they fade out.

A short time after they thought they've established a new routine they can stick to, they give up and go back to their pre-makeover selves, which can mean no makeup at all or makeup done in all the wrong ways. In some cases, it's not so much about a lack of effort or skill. They haven't yet established an appreciation for what a proper makeup routine can really do to their outer—and inner—selves because they haven't entered the beauty endorphin loop.

A lot of women don't know the power of beauty confidence because they've never experienced it. Makeup can be life-changing because it's confidence-changing. And let's be honest: On some days, makeup can be a lifesaver! Every one of us has watched a woman put on lipstick and stand a little taller. Granted, makeup isn't everything in the world. It won't promise you fame and fortune, a flatter belly, or that you'll live robustly to one hundred. But it can do things that a lot of other things can't. It's an inroad, an opportunity, a step in the right direction; it lifts your spirits, and is an asset accessible to all who dare to use it.

Every one of us needs something to help us sail through the day and make it better. Makeup has been that one instrument for me, and it can be yours, too. Even if you feel good about yourself and you consider yourself confident, there is nothing like feeling attractive and being positively recognized by others. In these pages I present to you the simplest, most comprehensive system for putting your best face on and achieving total beauty security and confidence. There are very few things in life that are instantly gratifying, empowering, and can trigger a greater sense of well-being in minutes. Every woman wants to look her best daily, but most don't think it's possible due to time constraints. The key is to know yourself and your Beauty I.D. (a concept we'll be exploring later on), follow the lessons in this book, and then sustain those new habits.

You will never have to search for another solution to your beauty routine again. Ever. You can do this, and you will succeed. In the end you'll only need to steal a few minutes from your day.

It all starts with the Gift of Time.

The Gift of Time

THE IMPORTANCE OF SELF-CARE
AND THE REWARDS OF TIME

The modern woman has a lot on her plate. I'll state the obvious: Women today straddle many competing demands between work and family life—and the increasing expectations to be "On" all the time and to respond quickly to every ping, call, email, and message. As young women are building careers, those a little older are often juggling kids and aging parents in addition to their work. At every age we feel the pressures of being caretakers and doers, and we tend to put ourselves last on the list. Some of us are not even on our own list anymore. It's normal to suddenly feel too swamped with responsibilities to bother taking an extra few minutes for intentional self-care.

While you understand the need to take care of yourself, at least theoretically, you tell yourself that you'll address it later when you're not so busy. But life is always abuzz and self-care perpetually gets cast aside. Some women use the "I'm too busy to take care of myself" as a badge of honor, as if it's something to be proud of. It's not. Neither is taking hours each morning getting ready but not really gaining anything of personal value out of that time. So if you're someone who already does make yourself a priority, my program will help you to optimize your time and gain the highest rewards.

What I mean by self-care goes beyond the basic essentials like eating and sleeping. I'm talking about investing quality time in activities that make you feel emotionally stronger, more self-confident, and secure. My goal in this book is to get you to perceive time a little differently. You have more than you realize, and if you use it well, you can cultivate the rewarding life you want and love—and look fabulous, too.

Minutes can be manna for the soul.

When I think about what I do, the term "makeup artist" doesn't occur to me first. Words like motivator, friend, teacher, mentor, and life coach come to mind. I have an awesome career; it's full of awe and wonderment that never ceases to inspire me. I can't imagine doing anything else, for makeup has made my dreams come true by giving me the ability to teach women the power of beauty confidence. And it has connected me to so many special people.

Every day I get to listen to women's stories—their challenges as well as their aspirations. The narratives share common themes: They all want to feel better about themselves and have a heightened sense of purpose, be more energized, experience more satisfaction and serenity and less stress or anxiety, and have less self-doubt and greater self-esteem. Time-starved but craving change, they don't know where or how to begin reaching these goals. But, like you, they intuitively know that if they looked prettier, they could gain an advantage. It's a stepping-stone in the right direction. The results I witness in their transformation are a constant source of inspiration.

Makeup's power is incredibly invigorating. The women I teach don't just leave my studio with longer-looking lashes and colorful lips. They walk away with brighter eyes and bigger smiles, while holding their heads higher. You see women on the street radiating these qualities, too, and you admire their beauty—a beauty that's an aura, less physical and more ethereal. Self-possessed, graceful, and seemingly unstoppable, they are ready to take on the day—and their lives—like never before. There is something to be said about comfort, too. When you're confident in your looks, you're comfortable. And when comfort emanates, you not only feel it but people sense it. It's alluring.

I've built a company around the truism that the path to a more fulfilling, meaningful life can begin with the Power of Makeup. It's why I am compelled to write this book: I know that if you invest a few minutes each day in front of the mirror, you'll be primed to pursue your best life. From my perspective, and from the thousands of women I've worked with who can attest to this fact, if you devote the time to polish your appearance, it will reflect back on how you regard and appreciate yourself. In other words, it's much more effortless—and more efficient—to work from the outside in.

In preparation for writing this book, my team and I decided to conduct a casual experiment. For two weeks, we asked women of all ages to take just a few minutes each day to engage in an activity focused on themselves that would boost their confidence for the day. For some, that was two minutes of silent meditation. For others, it was an extra fifteen minutes getting ready in the morning. We called it the Gift of Time. My goal was to get them to stack the deck in their favor through an intentional act that had the ultimate impact of setting themselves up for a more successful, productive day. At the end of the two weeks, these women filled out a questionnaire that would help us understand their experience. The results were shocking.

I had expected to discover that they enjoyed the experiment and wanted to keep spending an "extra" few minutes a day on themselves. But I never anticipated this: Every single woman—from the twenty-somethings to the sixty-somethings—admitted that they couldn't remember the last time they had taken a timeout to focus squarely on themselves: to have "me time." What's more, the mere minutes felt so transformative that it may as well have been two hours. Let me share some of the words these women used to describe the impact and effects of those few minutes:

more prepared for the day *luxurious*
grounded, centered, calmer *more accomplished*
more confident *excited for the day*
polished and pulled together *made me realize that I love me*
less frenzied

All of that for just a few minutes! The first question that came to mind upon reading the results was *why*? Why have we women gotten to a point where we don't take time to pay attention to ourselves? For if just a few minutes a day can bestow so many benefits on a woman, I say it's time to make this a nonnegotiable habit. While it's true that forces beyond your control can take away lots of things in your life, those forces cannot take away your freedom to choose how you spend your time and respond to situations.

We all know that a few minutes of self-care can make a favorable change in your attitude. And whether you are the CEO of a family or a company, you have the capacity each day to make that change for yourself. To spend dedicated time every morning in a manner that shifts your mood and outlook for the better. To routinely pursue activities that build confidence. The first step is to give yourself the Gift of Time.

I tell the women who visit me in my Manhattan studio that they need to make a two-week minimum commitment to taking that extra time for themselves every day so they can build this new habit into their lives. You can give me a few minutes. Better yet, you can give yourself a few minutes. There is so much promise.

If you're like many of the women I work with, you've been spending less and less time on yourself and are ready to pamper yourself with a new or upgraded skill set to look your best. Or perhaps you've never really had a good makeup routine and you're craving the professional skills. Some of the young women I meet have never established a trusty regimen that will help them enter adulthood with a bang and be ready for the world (and for the record, I show them the same application techniques as I do women three or four times their age; this system is ageless).

Whatever a woman's objectives are for working with me, she at least hopes to walk away from my makeup chair feeling as if she's exhaled some of her less confident self and is better prepared for—and excited about—the future. In all, she wants the kind of enhancement that ultimately helps her to begin a new chapter in her life that's filled with possibility. You can achieve the same result. And guess what:

It starts with beauty and cascades from there.

The Beauty Cascade

IT ALL STARTS HERE—THE RIPPLE EFFECT OF
LOOKING AND FEELING YOUR BEST

Let me ask you this:

- What does feeling secure in your appearance mean to you?

- When was the last time you took a moment from your regular (hectic) day to do something special just for you? How did it make you feel?

- How many times during the day or week do you love your looks and appreciate your body?

- Do you have any morning rituals that help you gain a head start on your day—an intentional habit that gives you an advantage and primes you for success no matter what the day may bring?

- How much confidence do you have on a daily basis? If you had more of it, what would you be able to achieve?

- What would life be like if you believed that you looked—and felt—your best every single day?

There is no vanity in taking advantage of makeup in order to get more of what you want in this world. Makeup is a tool—just like exercise classes are for staying in shape, or your car is to get you where you want to be. Any ambitious change has to start with one small step. And makeup can be that highly practical baby step that leads to a whole host of improvements. I call it the Beauty Cascade.

The minutes you spend in front of the mirror are about so much more than just applying makeup. By nudging yourself daily to put your best face on, you can profoundly shift your internal "makeup" and mindset. After all, attitude is everything, and getting into the right frame of mind can begin with simply beautifying yourself. Sometimes it only takes a few seconds and a little concealer to go from self-conscious to fully present. From insecure to confident. Makeup can allow you to discover yourself in ways you never thought possible. It facilitates the release of endorphins and can be your champion to the next level.

No sooner do you love what you see in your face in the mirror than your entire mentality changes and suddenly you're practicing other habits that culminate in a better, more beautiful you. By investing time in your beauty routine, you invest time in yourself, and those morning minutes become one of the most reliable and rewarding parts of the day.

Just as you probably have a different criteria for what it means to be "happy," your definition of "feeling your best" is unique to you, too. For me, feeling my best is knowing that I get to control my time, and that taking time for myself daily—no matter what's going on in my life—is essential.

Ask yourself: What does feeling *your* best mean? Maybe you wouldn't ordinarily include makeup in that definition, but I'm asking you right now to challenge yourself. Invest the time to put on your makeup using my system and see what happens. Start there and experience the benefits as they unfold. Looking your best is one of the easiest, most effective things you can do for yourself that yields high rewards. And those rewards will cascade quite effortlessly. Dedicate the time, and you will experience positive side effects in all aspects of your life.

Every single day offers renewal. We all make time for what's vital in our lives. At some point, though, you probably fell off your own list. It happens naturally when life gets hectic and in our way.

We abuse time. Yes, we are chronically immersed in To-Dos and our time is finite on this planet, but we have more time than we realize and appreciate. It's what Laura Vanderkam, author of *I Know How She Does It*, calls the busy person's lie: We tend to overestimate work hours and underestimate nonwork hours. Those nonwork hours could be better spent paying attention to and bettering ourselves. There are more minutes in the day than we imagine (1,440 to be exact) and more hours in the week (168). The average time that users spend on social media platforms is nearing an hour per day. That's more than any other leisure activity surveyed by the Bureau of Labor Statistics, with the exception of watching television programs and movies (an average of 2.8 hours). And it's almost as much time as people spend eating and drinking (1.07 hours). Good news: You can redefine how you view, measure, and manage your time, and therefore make more of it!

Maybe that still doesn't sound like a lot of time engaging in social media. But there are only 24 hours in a day, and the average person sleeps for about 7 of them. That means roughly one-seventeenth of the average user's waking time is spent on social media. (And yes, those companies work hard to find ways to keep you on their sites and apps and coming back for more.) In terms of the general media, adults in the United States consumed an entire hour more of media per day in 2016 than they did in 2015, and they spent 37 *more* minutes daily on their smartphones.

The fact that we're spending more than 50 minutes a day on social media says a lot. It says we're spending a lot of time looking at other people.

When you do turn away from the outside world for a moment and train your attention on just you, you can enter a self-perpetuating cycle of self-confidence that ultimately brings out the most beautiful you. It's not only electrifying, it's contagious. People will ask you what you've been up to. (They are thinking, I need some of that!)

It's not about having time. It's about making time.

Choice is powerful. We all have the ability to decide what we want and how we want to live, as well as the thoughts we choose to have. Not taking good care of yourself is just as much of an active choice as is taking excellent care of yourself. It cuts both ways. When I meet a woman who hasn't taken good care of herself, and she's clearly attuned to this fact but is finally seeking help, I will often ask directly: "When did you decide to not take care of yourself as you should?"

It's an important question that can relate to a lot of choices in life—when did you decide not to:

- Eat nutrient-dense, wholesome foods?
- Engage in regular physical activity that builds strength, stamina, and flexibility?
- Maintain activities and hobbies that fulfill you?
- Go after your dreams and goals with resolve?

Clearly these are rhetorical questions, but I think you get what I mean here. You've picked up this book with certain goals and aspirations in mind. You're ready.

Practically every day I run into women on the street who apologize for how they look, especially if they've left the house without any attention to their hair and makeup. "Oh, don't look at me! I look a mess. Sorry you have to see me like this!" It's like I've caught them naked. They feel the need to express regret, but it's not really directed at me. They are making the excuse to themselves. They know they could have done better and, as a result, *felt* better. There is beauty in every woman.

Life is nothing more than an endless series of choices. Some are relatively minor, such as where to go to dinner or what movie to see. Others are life-changing such as which career to pursue, whom to marry, and where to live. Once you think, choose, and act differently when it comes to your routines so that you maximize your confidence levels, you will be able to participate in life to its fullest.

I'm offering you an opportunity to leverage a few minutes of your morning to take ownership of yourself, your life, and your looks. Make YOU a priority. Whether you're going for the quick before-the-gym coverage or a full pre-date look, I will show you how to master my 8-step protocol to maximize your time and your beauty. Although I'm giving you the power of my 8-step program, in the end you may only use a few steps at a time. It simply depends on how much time you have and how many products you want to use.

Like so many other things in life, this is a process—a process I encourage you to stick to just as you would a diet to lose weight. But I promise that this will be much easier than any diet!

I promise that if you follow my program, you will reach the finish line shouting *I never knew I could look like this, I never knew looking my best was this easy, and I never knew I could feel this good.* All I ask from you at the start is to be open-minded, willing to experiment, and courageous enough to stand in your own beauty. I'll give you the basics you need to succeed. It'll be up to you to take it from there.

This book is about you. Begin to view your makeup routine as an indispensable component of self-care—right alongside those other requisite practices like exercise and healthy eating.

NOTHING MAKES A WOMAN MORE BEAUTIFUL THAN THE BELIEF THAT SHE IS BEAUTIFUL

– Sophia Loren

Trish McEvoy • BEAUTY
76 Perfect Foundation
Trish McEvoy • BEAUTY
65 Angled Contour
Trish McEvoy • BEAUTY
50 Angled Eye Lining
48 Sculpt and Blend
Trish McEvoy • BEAUTY
Wet/Dry Even Skin®
40 Medium Laydown
Trish McEvoy • BEAUTY
71 Perfect Face
Trish McEvoy • BEAUTY
Fan
Trish McEvoy • BEAUTY
Trish McEvoy • BEAUTY
Angled Crease Contour
Trish McEvoy • BEAUTY
5 Powder

Tools of the Trade

GET ORGANIZED: TAKE THAT SELFIE,
SIMPLIFY YOUR MAKEUP BAG, ESTABLISH A SKINCARE
ROUTINE, AND FIND YOUR MORNING MINUTES

Welcome to the training grounds. In this section, you're going to get organized. You'll take that makeup-less selfie, gather your brushes, learn a few skincare techniques, and find your morning face time.

Consider yourself lucky. There's been a revolution in the beauty industry, which has evolved rapidly in the past few years. Having been in the business for quite some time, something I've seen that's changed for the better is the quality of products available today. Foundations, for example, now blend smoothly into the skin so they don't cake or look like an added layer sitting on top. Current cosmetic technology overall is able to simulate nature, which enables less to be more: fewer products, fewer steps, and less time, with better results than ever. Handier tools have also made the application process much easier and with greater precision and perfection.

High-tech and low-tech treatments can enhance the appearance and texture of your skin, too, as well as diminish the appearance of fine lines and wrinkles. The combination of owning the right tools, knowing how to take care of your skin daily, leveraging special treatments that will further support your skin's health, and having a trusty makeup routine attuned to your personality and style is key to bringing out your beauty. I believe strongly in this synergy. It's what ultimately ushers out confidence.

Another shift that has occurred in the past decade or so has been the skincare industry's growth. It has been colossal, outpacing the women's fitness market. Why? People are becoming more informed about the value of taking care of their skin, especially in an era when we're all on social media and seflies are the norm. Speaking of which, I recommend we start there.

TAKE A MAKEUP-LESS SELFIE

Photographs are powerful, and can be much more so than a mirror in a lot of ways. When you're looking in the mirror, you're often feeling emotions in the reflection based on the kind of day you're having. Photographs, on the other hand, are more objective. Some people are more photogenic than others, but by and large photos show what the world sees.

Remove every ounce of makeup and then take a photograph of yourself. Make sure you have good lighting. Try different angles, too. This is your "before" shot. You are doing this so you have a record of yourself at the start—a way of measuring what you look like now before you take the plunge and follow through with my protocol. It's like getting on a scale before you commence a weight-loss diet. Do not fret over how this photo makes you feel. You do not have to show it to anyone.

The term "selfie" became part of the urban dictionary more than ten years ago, but it's nothing new. Self-portraits have been around for a long time, and they do impart benefits. You are capturing a memorable moment. This will help you to ultimately take full ownership of your looks—and yourself—and to improve upon both day after day.

LET'S GO PURSE DIVING

There's a great line in the movie *The Incredibles* spoken by the main character: "You know . . . you can tell a lot about a woman by the contents of her purse . . ." How true that statement is.

If I were to peek inside your purse right now, what would it say about you? Are you a neat freak who has everything organized and in its proper place, with nothing extra? Or are you the type to let things pile up and get a little messy and disorganized, with lots of extra things you don't need? I'm going to help you find your Beauty I.D. in the upcoming pages, but right now it helps to get up close and personal with *who* you are. And if you are the disorganized type, then it's time to adjust course. Do not wait for spring cleaning.

Anyone who knows me well knows that I like order. I'm obsessed with proper placement, and I admire organization in other people. I'm constantly on the lookout for a new tip that will make my life easier and prettier. People who are organized have one less thing to worry about. They are more calm.

I encourage you to take a good, honest look at your purse and do some cleaning out if necessary. This is part of your reboot. Ditch anything you don't truly need (or that's old, outdated, expired, or simply trash). Then go to your makeup bag (and drawer if you have one) and ruthlessly edit out old cosmetics. Throw away anything that smells funny, that you haven't used in a while, or that you just don't like. If you don't love it, lose it. In general, makeup has a shelf life of a year, with the exception of mascara, which should be replaced every three months. Make sure that your tools—the brushes, powder puffs, and sponges—are clean and in excellent condition. Sharpen your eye and lip pencils. If you can splurge on a new makeup bag or case, go ahead! Start fresh.

There are many types of makeup bags and cases. Be sure to find the storage system that works for you. Are you the type who takes makeup with you, or do you keep it all in your bathroom? Is it spread out on your vanity or packed in drawers—or both? Do you travel a lot? Do you need two sets of makeup bags? Whatever the *case* may be, your makeup carrier should be adaptable, flexible, functional, and attuned to your lifestyle. My favorite system is the one I designed, the patented Makeup Planner. Prompted by my makeup sprawl over a small hotel bathroom, my husband once said to me: "There has to be a better way." A sort of "portable makeup vanity," the Planner condenses the craze of makeup-filled countertops and drawers into a single compact, mirrored, zip-around case.

This system grew out of my need for order, structure, tidiness, and simplicity despite my need for options and love of choice. Whether at home or on the road, I wanted to be mobile and travel light, to save space and not have to open and close tons of compacts to find what I'm looking for. The Planner is simply that: a binder or book of makeup with "pages" that hold pans of colors I can see all at once. The pages are mirrored so you can even do your makeup on your lap. It also has brush sleeves so you can keep your colors and tools together at your fingertips. Personally, I keep one large Planner at home, a medium one packed and ready for travel, and a small Planner in my purse. This system works well for me.

Whatever system you choose—and please hear me on this—above all else, make sure that it *adds to* rather than *detracts from* your sense of calm and joy. That it enables you to get up and go when opportunity knocks. That it keeps your beauty uncompromised, whether you apply your makeup at home, on your commute, at the office, or all of the above. Don't allow disorder or unpreparedness to force you to skip the steps that make you feel good. Because isn't feeling good what this is all about? An organized system will free you up to enjoy your mirror time. This calm will cascade into whatever you are setting out to do.

SKIN CARE BASICS: THE FIVE ESSENTIALS

Your skin is among the most dynamic, ever-changing organs of your body. Skin is constantly evolving due to age; health; environment; hormones; and habits, including your diet and activities. To create and maintain a healthy radiance, you need to adhere to a daily routine while responding to your skin's shifting needs. If you see an unwelcome change in your skin, consider all aspects of your life: Has your climate changed—outside, or indoors through heat or air-conditioning—and have you adjusted your skincare and makeup accordingly? How have you been sleeping? Do you eat a nutritious diet and exercise regularly? Do you stay hydrated by drinking water throughout the day? Are you taking any medications that could be impacting your skin? In an emotional sense, how are your stress levels? All of these count and factor mightily into the skin equation.

I've learned a lot through my work with my dermatologist husband who cofounded with me one of the world's first medical spas. It was groundbreaking. The combination of a dermatologist and a beauty expert in one office fostered a tectonic shift in the way we approached beauty. No longer was beauty just about cosmetics. It was about so much more—blending science and art to teach women how to take care of their skin and bring out their best features, as well as encouraging them to ask questions. We wanted to elevate not only how women looked, but, more importantly, how they felt. For us, beauty also was about good health, a reflection of the entire self and one's overall well-being.

Our philosophy has always been results-oriented. Such results are evermore easy to achieve with today's technologies and given what we know about how best to take care of skin. Following some basic guidelines can make a world of difference in the skin's short- and long-term beauty and health. The five daily skincare steps are:

- Cleanse
- Exfoliate
- Moisturize
- Protect
- Repair

SKIN TYPE TEST

1. Wash your face with a gentle wash.

2. Wait 15 minutes.

3. Assess your skin. If it is:

IRRITATED: You have sensitive skin.

TIGHT: You have dry skin.

BALANCED: You have normal skin.

SHINY ALL OVER: You have oily skin.

SHINY ON THE T-ZONE (central part of the face, including forehead, nose, and chin)**:** You have combination skin.

STEP 1. CLEANSE

Cleansing is the fresh start you give skin at the beginning and end of each day. It is the best time investment you can make in your beauty, and vital to your skin's clarity, balance, and health. This is particularly important before going to bed after a day's accumulation of makeup, oils, and environmental debris. Choose a multifunction cleanser that removes eye and face makeup while cleansing the skin and preserving its natural balance. Consider the texture of cleanser that feels best on your skin. If you have oily skin to begin with, you may like the fresh feel of a gently foaming wash formula. For drier skin, use a product with a balm or milky texture. For times you're unable to get to a sink, the French micellar technology of cleansing waters, which gently emulsify even long-wear makeup, enables you to take it all off without the need to rinse.

When you are washing your face at the sink, my most important pointer is to rinse well. Many people think they are rinsing well when they are, in fact, creating problems by splashing too lightly and leaving behind traces of makeup and cleanser. The advice I have given throughout my career is to cup your hands and saturate your face at least ten times. This will ensure you receive a thorough cleanse.

STEP 2. EXFOLIATE

Until the age of about twenty-five, dead skin cells turn over, i.e., shed, at a high rate. As we age, this turnover slows down and we need to boost the process with exfoliation. If you don't, dead cells will gather and you'll end up with dull-looking skin.

Exfoliation uncovers smooth, radiant new skin and enables your skincare to better absorb. It reduces breakouts and hastens their recovery. It will also allow your makeup to look smooth—as if it is part of, not on top of, your skin. Last but not least, it reduces the appearance of lines, wrinkles, pores, and even dark spots over time.

I recommend exfoliating each or every other day. You may want to try different methods.

CHEMICAL VS. MANUAL

A chemical exfoliant could be an alpha hydroxy acid (AHA) or beta hydroxy acid (BHA) wash. These are acid-containing formulas that chemically exfoliate by dissolving the dead cells. BHAs are the most gentle form of chemical exfoliation.

Masks and scrubs have been around forever, and they manually, rather than chemically, exfoliate the skin. Look for natural ingredients like jojoba beads, sea salt, and sugar.

STEP 3. MOISTURIZE

There's no quicker way to ensure your skin is soft and glowing than to hydrate it. The most effective way to hydrate your skin is with a hyaluronic acid–rich serum or cream. Hyaluronic acid is a moisture magnet, proven to improve the skin's moisture barrier. Depending on how your skin feels, a serum or cream alone may be enough. On dryer days, you may want to layer serum and cream together.

If you are not familiar with or do not understand the serum/essence world, you should know the role they play. Often as light as water, serums and essences are highly concentrated nutrient infusions that absorb quickly and can address an array of concerns, while offering immediate as well as long-term treatment benefits. Serums not only improve the skin's beauty and health, they also boost the performance of your other skincare products.

Creams, on the other hand, have a richer texture and can work beautifully alone or over serum. An effective cream will deliver and lock water into the skin, temporarily plump up fine lines, and soften the skin's appearance. Choose a formula for your skin type. If you have normal, combination, or oily skin, look for a lightweight moisturizer. If you tend to be on the drier side, seek a creamier formula. Ensure that your moisturizer absorbs quickly and gives your skin a smooth pre-makeup finish. You may want to choose a multifunction formula that also contains sunscreen and/or offers coverage, which will speed up your routine and cut down the number of steps. When using more than one face product, remember to always apply the thinnest first.

STEP 4. PROTECT

In this day and age, we have all heard endless warnings about the imperative role sunscreen plays in our beauty and health. They are all correct: Sunscreen is an important factor in cancer prevention and how your skin ages. When picking a sunscreen, only consider options that claim UVA/UVB or broad-spectrum protection. As my husband always told his patients, when it comes to UV damage, A is for the rays that Age and B is for those that Burn. You want to block them both. At a minimum, choose a sunscreen with an SPF of 30 and use it every single day, whether it's sunny or not. Many of today's moisturizers come with SPF already built in. As noted above, it's fine to use a product that acts as both a moisturizer and a sunscreen, which you apply before your makeup. Take care to use a generous amount, and cover all exposed skin. If you're sensitive to the chemical-based sunscreens, look for formulas that use titanium or zinc dioxide, which create a physical barrier and do not penetrate the skin. Whatever you choose, think of your sun care as a beauty retirement account; your future self will thank you!

STEP 5. REPAIR

Your skin goes through a lot each day. To help counteract the daily environmental toll, each night it is important to boost your "beauty sleep"—a term that comes from the repair state our bodies enter when we sleep—with reparative treatments that will make the most of every resting minute. Evening is prime time for your retinol and moisture masks, as well as vitamin C treatments, at-home peels, or any other treatments that increase the skin's sensitivity to the sun.

INGREDIENTS THAT MAKE
A DIFFERENCE

When selecting your skincare products to cover the five essential steps, it is a bonus if they contain any of the following powerhouse ingredients that have stood the test of time and are truly proven to make a difference:

AHAs (alpha hydroxy acids)**:** Break up dead/dull skin cells and encourage cellular renewal. Glycolic acid is the most common AHA. It's the most effective at improving the overall appearance of the skin. Note: This can be irritating to people with sensitive skin types. Glycolic acids have small molecules, so they penetrate the skin deeply and can also stimulate collagen production.

BHAs (beta hydroxy acids)**:** Or salicylic acids, are slightly milder than AHAs and typically used to target acne and clear pores, in addition to improving skin tone and reducing inflammation.

HYALURONIC ACID: A moisture magnet that instantly boosts the skin's hydration and ability to retain moisture over time.

PEPTIDES: Support natural collagen production while helping to resist environmental damage.

ANTIOXIDANTS: Disarm free radicals—rogue molecules that have lost an electron and can damage cells and tissues—so they cannot inflict harm. In the skin, free radicals can arise from exposure to irritants such as UV rays and environmental pollutants, including tobacco smoke and general air pollution. Many of today's beauty products will advertise for their antioxidant ingredients, but two in particular are deserving of your attention: vitamin C and derivatives of vitamin A.

VITAMIN C: While you may think about vitamin C in terms of boosting your immune system, this antioxidant has many properties that aid in skin health, too. It stimulates the production of collagen and elastin—two main ingredients in skin that help keep it youthful and supple. In partnership with sun protection, vitamin C can help resist and repair signs of sun damage by helping to even, brighten, and tighten skin. Look for vitamin C–infused products, such as moisturizers and serums, that contain the vitamin in the form of L-ascorbic acid, which has been shown to be the most effective. Because it increases the skin's sensitivity to the sun, apply vitamin C at night and wear sunscreen by day.

RETINOL/VITAMIN A: Stimulates the natural production of healthy collagen while protecting against the aging process. The vitamin A family has long been shown to help address skincare problems, especially accumulated sun damage and acne. Retin-A is by prescription only, but many over-the-counter products contain weaker forms of the derivative that will give you the same results but take longer. Look for the words retinol, retinyl acetate, retinyl linoleate, or retinyl palmitate. You may experience some skin irritation in the form of redness and flakiness when you begin using these products, and that is normal. You can start small, using a retinol-infused product, for example, twice a week and bump up your usage as your skin gets used to it. Be sure to use plenty of sunscreen when you begin using these products because they can make your skin more sensitive to sunlight.

Makeup is a science and an art, which means it requires the proper instruments to do it right. My favorite tools are my brushes. After all, they are what got me into this business. Early on in my career, I created my own set by reshaping brushes I bought at the art store. They made putting on makeup easier, simpler, and quicker.

My entire application process changed—it was the beginning of a disruptive innovation that would affect the entire beauty industry. Suddenly, I was gaining control of makeup like never before and others would benefit. And as I've always said, "Your choice of brushes determines the look you achieve."

It's up to you how many brushes you want to own and maintain. Whether you are someone who wants just a few multifunctional brushes or an infinite number of tools, having the right high-quality brushes that you can afford for each step in your makeup routine will make it easy for you to consistently achieve the best results. The brushes will do the work for you. They are as important a purchase as the makeup you choose.

All brushes should be washed once a week and wiped cleaned after every use. I like to spray mine after each use with brush cleaner. To wash, use gentle shampoo formulated for brushes. Put a dollop in your palm and gently swish the brush in your hand. Avoid getting the metal ferrule wet or the bristles will shed. After washing, rinse in clean water and press out the excess moisture with a towel. Lay the brush flat over the edge of a smooth surface with the head hanging over so that air can reach the bristles. Also remember: You will get more definition with shorter bristles.

Other tools will also be essential to your success. Here are the must-haves that maximize my makeup application and time:

COTTON SWABS: Look for a duel-ended swab, one side with a pointed tip for detail work and the other side with a flat, rounded head for blending and/or makeup removal.

SPONGES: These are very important tools. They ensure your makeup is well blended, they press the product into the skin to give it a more professional look, and they come in many different shapes and sizes. The key here is to look for sponges that have a flat side as well as a pointed edge.

PUFFS: Powder puffs are textured for expert control and even application of pressed and loose powder products. They are designed to blend out lines of demarcation for a seamless face-color application.

PENCIL SHARPENER: How else do you plan to sharpen your eyeliner? I prefer a sharpener that holds the shavings for easy cleanup, and so I can sharpen anywhere.

EYELASH CURLER: Lash curlers are designed to create optimal lift and curl. I prefer the ones that are curved and have rounded rubber pads.

TWEEZERS: To get those wayward hairs, you'll need a good pair of tweezers. Look for the ones that give you a good grip.

MIRROR: Although any bathroom mirror with good lighting can work for you, I think every woman should have a mounted or standing mirror that has a light, tilts, and has one magnified side. A mirror that tilts allows you to get much closer for eye makeup, where details matter. You'll want to be able to lift your chin and look down with your eyelids flat. This position is much easier to achieve with a mirror that's slightly tilted. Natural daylight is your perfect source, but a lighted mirror allows you to see everything more precisely.

BEAUTY IS SELF-CONFIDENCE APPLIED DIRECTLY TO THE FACE

– Anonymous

Bent eyelining brushes let you see your lash line while you work.

Small eye brushes offer maximum versatility from shadow to liner.

Angled eyelining brushes make it easy to get a perfect wing.

Flat-topped eyelining brushes foster precise, even lines.

Short, densely packed brushes smudge with precision.

Small sable-haired brushes conceal and add shadow with detail.

Full shadow brushes deliver a wash of color and blend.

Loose tapered shadow brushes create a soft crease contour.

Dense angled shadow brushes create a precise, deep contour.

Large shadow brushes quickly apply a wash of color.

Nylon laydown brushes deliver seamless medium-to-full cream or liquid coverage.

Sable laydown brushes are the all-in-one eye brush, great for creams, powders, shadows, and concealers.

Large laydown brushes are multifunctional face brushes, ideal for applying and blending creams, powders, and concealers.

Large flat-topped nylon brushes deliver a perfect
sheer application of cream and liquid products.

Densely packed rounded brushes deliver medium-to-full-
coverage application of foundation without absorbing product.

Densely packed flat-topped brushes deliver
seamless full-coverage application of foundation.

Dense tapered nylon brushes are perfect for contouring
and highlighting with creams, liquids, and powders.

Angled brushes deliver perfect contouring with powders and creams.

Large round-topped brushes are ideal for sheer powder application and setting your look with translucent powder. They are also key for blending.

Large fluffy tapered brushes deliver a sheer application of bronzer or finishing powder over the facial structure.

Small tapered brushes precisely apply face color and are great for detailed highlighting work.

Soft flat brushes apply the perfect detailed blush application.

Fan brushes apply a veil of face color and translucent powder.

Petite kabuki brushes precisely apply color to smaller contours of the face.

Multifunctional kabuki face brushes are ideal for contouring and applying bronzer and blush.

Concealer brushes let you apply color
with exact precision and control.
They can also be used as lip brushes.

Brow combs groom brows for
even color and shape. They will
also expose any out-of-place
hairs that need to be removed.

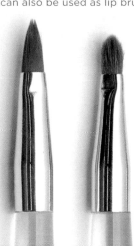

Trish McEvoy • BEAUTY
44 Precision Concealer

Trish McEvoy • BEAUTY
18 Detail

Trish McEvoy • BEAUTY
Brow Groomer

FIND YOUR MORNING MINUTES

Your mornings probably follow a similar pattern most days of the week. There's a typical time you wake up and get out of bed. Then you have a set of tasks to complete that you move through mindlessly. Everything feels down to the second. Finding an extra ten minutes or so might seem impossible, but not if you examine how you spend each of those minutes. Track yourself for a couple of days and identify what eats up your morning. You'd likely soon find that many minutes go to waste doing things that are low priority and can wait, or that don't help you gain a head start for yourself personally.

WHEN TO SEE A DERMATOLOGIST

Seeing a dermatologist at least once each year is just as important as your other annual exams. Every woman should visit a dermatologist annually for a full-body check for skin cancer. This is also a good time to review your skin beauty questions. The number of in-office treatments available today that can help address a wide array of skin issues is mind-boggling: chemical peels; and the use of revolutionary (and affordable) technologies like fractional and light treatments, such as Pixel skin resurfacing, which rejuvenates skin texture, and IPL (Intense Pulsed Light) photorejuvenation, which evens out skin tone. Many of these treatments require little or no downtime and can make a huge difference in your looks without going to extremes. And be vain! Don't feel awkward about asking what could be good for you and your skin, particularly if you suffer from a skin issue or condition that bothers you. Just remember: Moderation is key; too much of anything—injectables, plastic surgery, even too much makeup—can have the opposite of your intended effect and make you look older or even downright funny!

The time you take to put your best face on can be the smallest commitment for the biggest payoff. Think of those personal minutes as vitamins. They are crucial to your entire being and biology. I don't care whether you're the two-minute lip-gloss girl or the woman who takes twenty minutes to perfect her eyeliner and shadow; the key is to take the time. Be intentional.

If the thought of finding a pocket of time in the morning to take the makeup challenge is already causing panic, let me offer some suggestions. This is easier than you think if you scrutinize what you did just this morning and are able to realize where you could have created some shortcuts or eliminated nonessential tasks. There might be a necessary chore that could be moved to the night before (e.g., making the kids' lunches, laying out what you'll wear the following day, organizing your bag). Maybe getting up fifteen minutes earlier is the solution, which won't ruin a good night's sleep. Prioritize your makeup routine as you would other morning essentials so that it's not ignored or pushed aside and you're not applying your mascara in the car. Set a reminder on your phone to alert you at a time you know you can commit to every day for the next two weeks (e.g., 7:15 a.m.). If the timing is not consistent each day, that's okay. But figure out the night before what time will work for you the next morning and commit to that. Again, be intentional.

To stay motivated, write down three reasons for doing this. Here's a helpful question to ask yourself for ideas: If an opportunity presented itself today (e.g., meeting someone new, being offered a raise or new job), how do you want to look and feel? Another idea is to post a note on the bathroom mirror for inspiration:

Did you take your morning minutes today?

WHAT'S YOUR MORNING STYLE?

Everyone has a morning method. Not every day is exactly the same, but in general we each have our patterns that match our personalities and needs (early riser? snoozer?). Below are common themes to typical morning styles. There is nothing wrong with any one of these approaches, but it helps to be mindful of how they play into whether or not you can find your morning minutes and use them with intention.

THE PROCRASTINATOR

This woman is a frenetic tornado of activity in the morning, hitting the snooze until the last possible moment, diving headlong through the shower, cursing at sleeping in, and scrambling to get out the door as fast as possible.

SOLUTION: Get up 15 minutes earlier. If it's too difficult to do this without extra help, find motivators. Have really good coffee available; put on some music to inspire you ("aural coffee").

THE MULTITASKER

This woman is doing a million things right from the get-go, and most of them are not for herself. Whether it's getting kids out the door to school, fielding calls from family and friends, checking in on social media, caring for pets, or triaging the email inbox, the morning flies by without more than a second or two of thought on herself.

SOLUTION: Perform tasks the night before that don't have to be done in the morning (e.g., pack your bag, make kids' lunches, perform general household chores).

THE AUTOPILOT

This woman's morning runs with military precision. She has her routine down pat from the second she gets out of bed until she walks out the door so that she can do it without thinking and know that she's put together and has what she needs.

SOLUTION: Be intentional about your time rather than just going through the motions. Avoid any unnecessary tasks, media, or phone calls even if you think you can fit them into your routine. By treating those morning moments—especially the ones in front of the mirror—with extra care, you'll feel more empowered and ready to face the day.

Additional strategies to save time:

- Do not check email, Internet, or social media before putting on your makeup.
- Let calls go to voicemail so you can choose whom to call back, if necessary, once out the door.
- Write out your To-dos the night before.
- Tidy up the kitchen the night before so you're not wasting fifteen minutes there in the morning.
- Have an Essentials List that includes the three or four things you want to accomplish in the morning, and include your time in front of the mirror.

Although every day is a little different, I do plan my days well and stick to the same morning habits. On a typical day I am up at 5:00 a.m. I start on a positive note with coffee, music, and by setting the atmosphere through scent. I have my oatmeal and download *Women's Wear Daily* and the *Wall Street Journal*. On most mornings I get on the treadmill for half an hour. (I aim to move every day, be it walking or formal exercise, and make sure to move throughout the day.) Then I shower and think about how I want to look that day. By 7:30 I'm hopping on a morning call and reviewing notes for work. I'm at the office between 8:30 and 9:00, where I sit with my team and go over what has to get done that day.

The women in my office each have their own morning routines, and no two are identical. They do what they need to arrive feeling ready, prepared, and presentable. For Cassandra, for example, who has two young children, she does the least she can get away with and doesn't spend a lot of time on her makeup. For Rosa, on the other hand, her morning method is extensive (she uses lots of products) but nevertheless time efficient.

The organization of your time in the morning will set you up for a successful day. So many women let time run them over rather than gaining control of it and using it wisely. What will it take for you to take charge of your morning for just yourself? I realize that we all have our obligations that can get in the way of our good intentions, such as young children who need our attention or an unexpected work emergency that has us running out the door quickly. But do what you can to make yourself a priority.

I recommend buying a calendar or day planner if you don't already have one. I love my calendar. It helps me stay focused and organized. I know what's coming up and where I need to put my energy. The time I spend with my calendar is nonnegotiable: both the month-at-a-glance and daily sections. Use your preferred method of planning to map out your time and responsibilities, especially on training grounds in the next two weeks. Be clear not only about your morning minutes, but your entire day.

Keep asking yourself:
What do I need to make my day work?

Sometimes it feels impractical and selfish to focus on your life when a demanding job or family obligations take up a lot of your time and energy. This is when it's important to remember that you are in charge of your life—and your beauty. You get to choose. And with the right tools, you can make a difference that carries you to a place where you're calmer, happier, and more confident.

In the next pages, you're going to learn how to identify which Level you are. Your Level determines which makeup and application techniques you choose. While we can certainly switch up the Levels we choose based on what kind of day is ahead of us, most of us have a signature style—a trusty Level—that we stick to at least 80 percent of the time. That's the look in which we feel most comfortable.

So which Level are you? Time to discover your Beauty I.D. and then establish a plan of action for utilizing those minutes.

Discover Your Beauty I.D.

FIND YOUR EVERYDAY LEVEL (1, 2, OR 3)
AND LEARN WHAT KIND OF BEAUTY
ADVOCATE YOU WANT TO BE FOR YOURSELF

If I were to ask you about your "style," what would you say? It probably changes on a daily basis depending on what you're doing, but you likely have a basic style that embodies you most of the time. A lot of things factor into a woman's style: type of job, is she a student, whether or not she's a mother to young children, time constraints, age, tastes and preferences, and even geography. If you were to come see me for a consultation, I'd ask you a series of questions that help me get a sense of who you are so I can then customize your experience and beauty regimen.

I meet a lot of women who seek a new look because they feel that they have outgrown their current one. Your Level determines which makeup and application techniques you choose.

Think about the following three questions:

- How much time do you have to apply your makeup?
- How many products do you use?
- Would you leave the house without your makeup on?

Now, which Level best describes you 80 percent of the time? The Levels are a factor of time and attention to details. Some women can spend twenty minutes to get the "all-natural" look, whereas others can glam themselves up in dramatic fashion relatively quickly. A Level 1 girl could have no foundation, no eye makeup, but a dramatic red lip!

LEVEL 1: You don't take a lot of time getting ready and applying makeup. You want to put it on and go, using just a few products, and may even skip makeup entirely on some days. Your makeup routine is basic, but it's still important to you.

LEVEL 2: Most women fall into this category. You rely on makeup daily to enhance and define your look. You won't leave the house without it. You use an array of products, and makeup is an important factor in your life.

LEVEL 3: You love what makeup can do for you. It's already a nonnegotiable—a creative journey. You devote quality time to your makeup routine and are not afraid to be bold and daring with your finished, well-defined look. Your makeup bag is extensive and comprehensive and you tend to have extra products in your purse. All of us can be Level 3s at various moments, such as on our wedding day or a milestone birthday, but a lot of women like this look daily.

These Levels have nothing to do with age, but they can change over time or given certain circumstances. As I mentioned, the Levels are more a factor of time, lifestyle, and how many products you want to use. It helps to think of them as progressive steps. You can also be a Level 1 for 80 percent of the time, and bump up to a Level 2 for a special occasion. Similarly, a Level 2 might scale down to a Level 1 over the weekend, or go up to a Level 3 for an evening affair. You can build from a Level 1 to a Level 3 without starting off with a bare face.

So think about which Level you are today. It's a vehicle through which you become your own beauty advocate. You don't have to limit yourself to that Level forever. But at least be clear about which Level reflects you best going forward. Remember, your Level is defined by your general approach to makeup; it is not an absolute.

BEAUTY DOESN'T STOP AT THE FACE

We all intuitively know that beauty—and overall well-being in general—is an outcome of innumerable facets. It also is imbued with complexity and nuances. I like to say that beauty is in the details. This includes everything from the right hairstyle and wardrobe to the right amount of sleep and exercise, and even the right attitude.

Beyond makeup, what else do you need to feel—and look—your best? Think about the little things you do for yourself unrelated to cosmetics that put a smile on your face. Those little things count whether it be a new haircut and highlights, or even reading a great book. Nourishing your beauty and interests are every bit as much a part of how you become your own beauty advocate.

Part of becoming your own beauty advocate entails finding which habits will play into a healthy sense of self and making sure you don't abandon them. I have a friend, for example, who is an avid runner and cycler. She calls her exercise routine her "church" and has to do something that breaks a sweat daily or she doesn't feel right and her self-confidence begins to wane. Her entire day, in fact, often revolves around her rigorous exercise routine. On the days when she's really tired and actually thinks about skipping her run or cycle, she reminds herself about how great she'll feel on the other side of the workout and that alone is enough to motivate her. She employs the power of visualization to get moving.

I have another friend who struggles with finding time to exercise but knows that it's important for her overall health. So what does she do? She doesn't keep a hair dryer or shampoo at home. This forces her to go to the gym in the morning and get ready for work there after time on the elliptical machine. There's nothing wrong with tricking yourself into keeping up with the habits that you know will increase your health and well-being, as well as factor into your beauty equation. But you have to do the work. I lost twenty pounds when I cut out frappuccinos and bought a Fitbit. Those were my tricks. What will yours be in your quest to become your own beauty, and by extension, health advocate? What will it take to look and feel your best?

A FEW WORDS ABOUT JOURNALING

Self-care and self-discovery go hand in hand. And committing your thoughts and ideas to paper can make a huge difference. It provides a record for you, while simultaneously offering accountability and a heightened sense of self-awareness. It also gives you a chance to adjust your attitude if need be and set a new course. So few of us take dedicated time during the day to press pause on everyone and everything else and just sit and think in our own creative, calm head.

Write down your short-term To-dos and indicate the time you'll find for your morning minutes. Also, keep track of your long-term goals. And don't forget to note all the good things that happen for which you're grateful. There's scientific data now to show that gratitude can indeed trigger positive health effects. The more grateful we feel, the more resilient the brain becomes, physically and even emotionally and spiritually. At the end of the day—even the most stressful of days— stop and reflect: *What actually went right? What am I thankful for? What good came out of the day, even if it was unplanned or unexpected?* I like to relive successes and special moments in my evenings, and digest what I could have done differently or better. This touch-base with myself gives me a sense of peace and control that, like my mirror time in the morning, cascades positivity into the rest of my life. Sometimes, on the worst of days, we can just be thankful that we got through it, and soon we can embrace a whole new day with happy, promising thoughts and intentions.

8 Steps
to Exceptional

DETAILED AND EASY-TO-FOLLOW TUTORIALS

Here you are. Organized. Equipped. Ready to go. You have a better sense of who you are and what goals you'd like to achieve. You understand your Beauty I.D. and how to be your own beauty advocate. Now it's time to roll up your sleeves and learn how to fine-tune your looks using simple tools and strategies. This comes from pure knowledge—knowing what to do and how to do it. I will show you how to discover your own makeup style, follow an effortless sequence you can rely on, and customize your regimen. With the proper methods, I trust you will have what you need to realize the strength in your beauty.

A new habit takes time and practice to establish. Make it a goal to go through all 8 steps daily over the next two weeks, even if you ultimately choose to use just a few of these steps. Commit to fourteen days of putting your face on whether you leave the house or not. It will have the impact of not only building this new routine into your day, but it will also help you master the steps quickly. You'll be putting on makeup like a professional soon enough. Make the most of your morning minutes over the next two weeks as you teach yourself these important lessons and tune in to how you are feeling as you up-level your looks. You will be rebooting your appearance and your attitude one day and one makeup application at a time. You'll start to see results immediately, and even more will accumulate over time as you stay the course.

THE GROUND RULES

The following guidelines work for any Level. Follow these before you begin the application process:

ALL TOGETHER NOW: Don't wait until your application is underway to go looking for brushes, cotton swabs, and your favorite eye shadow. Have everything right in front of you, all spread out and organized in a fashion that's convenient for quick application. Remove any clutter.

SET THE STAGE: Before any makeup touches your face, prep it with moisturizer, eye cream, and lip balm. Give your skin a minute or two to absorb them. Blot away any excess preparation product with a tissue.

TIP: Ideally, use a magnifying mirror to put on your makeup, especially when you apply your eye makeup. Makeup that looks good magnified looks even better from a distance. Also, if you use your fingertips, tap and press. Do not push and rub. When only one finger is needed, use your ring finger—it's your weakest finger and will ensure you press lightly. Otherwise, use a brush.

BLENDING BLUNDER: If you don't blend well enough when it comes to your foundation, concealer, blush, and bronzer, you'll expose telltale edges. It's one of the most common mistakes I see. Blend! Blend! Blend! Use a wet sponge or a big puff to help soften the effect. I will be reminding you to blend and powder throughout the application process.

EYE START: In the past you might have started with foundation and concealer first. I like to start with the eyes. As you dress your eyes, product can fall onto your face. It's much easier to clean up any fallen product before you've put on foundation, concealer, or powder. When applying upper eye makeup, it helps to lift your chin and look down into the mirror (which is why a magnifying mirror that tilts is a big help). This allows you to create a flat lid while still being able to see what you're doing. Avoid squinting, as this can lead to applying makeup to wrinkles and folds. When applying to the lower eye, put your chin down and look up into the mirror.

TAKE ANOTHER SELFIE

When you are done with your 8 steps, take another photograph of your face in attractive lighting. Create a record—and a memory—of how you look now. Keep this picture handy for when you don't feel inspired to put your best face on. You can print a copy and tape it to your bathroom mirror if you like. Set it beside the "before" photo. Celebrate the transformation. Don't forget it!

REGULAR ASSESSMENTS

As the seasons change, our wardrobe changes. You don't have to feel the need to change your Level unless your time and preferences change. And remember, the Levels have nothing to do with your age. That said, I recommend that you assess your makeup needs on a regular basis and make basic adjustments. You can also do this weekly or monthly depending on what's going on in your life. But at least try to find a regular beat in your life where it makes sense to stop and take an honest look at yourself in the mirror. Those beats can be when you get your hair cut, for example, or when you transfer certain pieces of clothing out of your closet and into storage for the seasonal change. You may move through acutely stressful periods, for example, that demand more definition to your makeup routine. If you have a series of bad nights' sleep for whatever reason, it helps to pay more attention to coverage, concealer, and eye details. You'd be surprised by what an extra step or two in your beauty routine can do to address common problems.

Below is my list of top problems most women face at some point, and how to address them:

ON THE DAYS YOU'RE SERIOUSLY UNDERSLEPT: Sleep deprivation can be erased from your face if you focus on lightening any shadowy areas and adding subtle touches of brightness to your complexion and lips. Start by blending a lightening and brightening product over dark areas, especially under the eyes and in the nasolabial folds around your mouth. I'm a big believer in the technique called Triangle of Light. This allows maximum brightening, alleviating the look of fatigue. Apply rosy blush to the apples of your cheeks and use a slightly brighter, translucent lip color. Avoid opaques on tired skin. Do a light dusting of bronzing powder and don't forget mascara. Mascara is eye-opening magic on a face that's tired underneath it all!

ON THE DAYS YOU'RE RECOVERING FROM A LATE-NIGHT DINNER OR PARTY: Hydrate from the inside out and outside in. Drink a tall glass of water and exfoliate before moisturizing your face. Exfoliation will help your skincare products better absorb. Address any dark circles. Use some bronzer or blush to brighten up your complexion and reach for the sheer lip color.

ON THE DAYS THE MIRROR GREETS YOU WITH A BIG UGLY BLEMISH: First and foremost, do not pick! Never pick a pimple or blemish, as that will make things worse and add days—sometimes weeks—to the healing process. Dab an anti-acne drying agent or medication directly onto the pimple using a cotton swab. Wait for it to dry, then apply concealer on top of the blemish with a tiny brush. Work it around in a one-centimeter-wide radius, then take a cotton swab and buff away the edges. Set with a touch of powder. Don't think about the blemish or stare at it in the mirror. Let it go away on its own. And again, don't touch it!

MAKE DOWN

When you go from work to play—let's say you're leaving your office for a casual get-together with friends—you might want to tone down your makeup. If your eyes are well-defined with dark liner, smudge a little off with a cotton swab. Using a puff, blend down your foundation and blush to the bare minimum of coverage. Finally, rather than reapply the same lipstick, especially if it's dark, stain your lips instead with a fresh-looking gloss.

MAKE UP

Rarely does one get the opportunity to spend an hour at home to transition between the day and an evening affair. Most of us scurry from place to place and do our best to get ready somewhere in between—at the desk, in the office or destination bathroom, or in the car. If you have the tools and time to start your makeup from scratch, by all means do so. But if you don't, you'll be fine just by adding more definition to the areas on which you want to focus: Touch up your eyeliner, add more shadow and blush, and take your lip color up a notch. For me, I also love to spritz on some fragrance. It instantly gets me into an evening mood.

SET THE MOOD

To me, scent is one of the great joys in life. Not only can it transform your mood, it can teleport you to a beloved time or place. My love affair with fragrance began at a very young age, when I often visited my grandmother's parfumerie. The scent memories of those years, and of many precious moments from throughout my life, can come rushing back to me with the opening of an aromatic bottle.

Spritzing myself before I apply my makeup is an integral part of my daily beauty experience and personal time. It slows me down and reminds me to stop and smell . . . LIFE! It helps me set the mood I want to feel and project to the world. I call fragrance the "invisible accessory" and believe it is as influential to our insides as skincare and makeup is to our outsides.

This passion translates to my fragrance-making approach, which is more spiritual than literal: When creating my most famous original scent, I gave the perfumer, who happened to be female, cues like "happy," "joyful," "uplifting." The result was unlike anything the fragrance world had experienced before, and it became a global bestseller. When I set out to create a sexy companion to this scent, I intentionally chose a male perfumer to get a man's perspective on the same theme. The fragrance bottle is also important to me: It must feel wonderful in your hand and look beautiful in your home. All these details lend to the great joy of the fragrance experience.

THE 8 STEPS

You can be your own professional makeup artist every day. All it takes is a little time and technique. Beauty—and confidence—starts here. In the upcoming pages you'll find a gallery of five women showing you how to create the look of a Level 1, 2, and 3. Each profile begins with a Level 1. I recommend that you start there and then play with Levels 2 and 3 based on how much detail and definition you want to add to each feature.

There are eight key elements to any look—we call these "steps"—and each accomplishes a particular goal:

STEP 1: Brighten and Prime Upper Eyes
STEP 2: Eyeliner and Color
STEP 3: Lash Enhancement
STEP 4: Under Eyes
STEP 5: Even Skin
STEP 6: Face Color
STEP 7: Brow Enhancement
STEP 8: Lip Enhancement

Remember, the difference in the Levels is a factor of time and attention to detail, so you'll find that, depending on the look you want to achieve, not every step is required for each Level (and not everyone needs every step).

Practice makes perfect—
let's get started . . .

The Power of the Makeup Planner

Andjela

Brighten and Prime the Upper Eye

A. Apply upper-eye brightener and primer directly and liberally to the eyelid.

B. Blend quickly and evenly from lash line to eyebrow using a laydown brush.

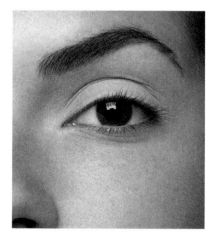

C. Sweep into the inner corner of the eye, what I call the "danger zone for darkness."

D. Ensure there are no missed spots and that you are seamlessly blended.

Eye Color and Lash Enhancement

A. Look down into the mirror with your chin up. Lift and hold your eyelid in place.

B. Dot a gel pencil at the base of the lashes, not on the waterline. This will create the look of a naturally full lash line

C. Place your mascara wand at the base of the lashes, then press and wiggle in a side-to-side motion up through the tips.

D. See how the lashes are well separated and gain a boost in volume.

Triangle of Light

A. Dot under-eye brightener in the shape of an upside-down triangle under each eye.

B. Extend the triangle down the length of the nose and up the cheekbone. Fill in the triangle with additional dots.

C. Gently press into the skin using a cream face brush.

D. Ensure you are well blended up to the lower lash line.

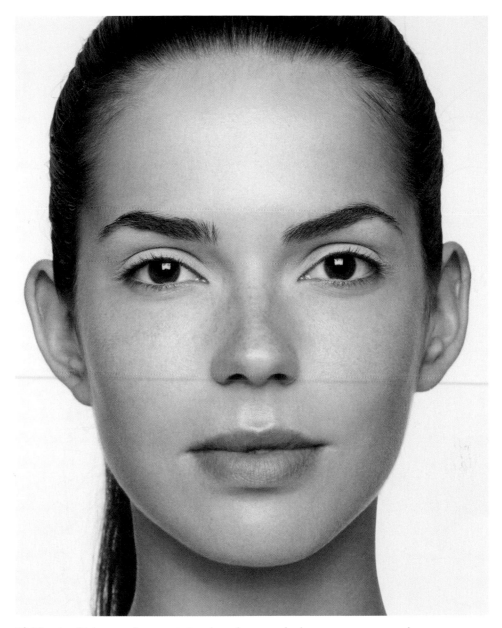

If, like Andjela, you have minimal under-eye darkness, you can apply dots of under-eye brightener as less coverage is necessary.

Even Skin and Face Color

A. Stipple foundation gently into the skin until perfectly blended.

B. Set and perfect foundation with powder.

C. Using circular motions, apply bronzer in a 3-shape, from hairline to cheekbone to jawline, at the sides of the face using a plush tapered brush.

D. Sweep from the center of the hairline to the temple to under the cheekbone to around the jawline.

After evening out your skin's tone, it is important to restore warmth and define the bone structure with bronzer.

Face Color

E. Apply blush to the apple of the cheeks. Blend out and down without bypassing the nose or eyebrows.

F. Set and perfect with translucent finishing powder using a fan brush.

Blush brightens the complexion for a look
of vibrant and healthy coloring.

Brow Enhancement and Lip Enhancement

A. If your brows are naturally full and well shaped, simply brush them into place following the direction of growth for a nicely groomed look.

B. If your lips are naturally full and well defined, simply add a hint of tint.

Eye Color

A. Press a brightening shadow across the lower lid.

B. Bring it up to the eyebrow.

C. Sweep a medium-toned shadow into the crease of the eye using a long tapered brush for a mistake-proof wash of color.

D. Press powder eye definer along the upper lashes using an angled eyelining brush.

E. Look into the mirror with your chin up. Gently press any remaining color along the lower lash line. Connect the upper and lower lash lines.

Lip Enhancement

To dress up your look and create the appearance of fuller lips, apply gloss to the center of your pout.

Eye Color

A. Apply a gently shimmering cream shadow along the lower lashes for soft definition.

B. Clean up the line using a precise, firm cotton swab.

C. Lay down a wing at the outer corner of the eye using a powder eye definer and angled eyelining brush.

D. Apply mascara to the lower lashes.

See the uplifting power of the wing!

Lip Enhancement

A. Invisibly outline the center of the lips with a brightener to naturally articulate their shape.

B. When applying bright or deep lip color, always use a lip brush for a precise yet soft look.

Lauren

Brighten and Prime the Upper Eye

A. Apply brightening shadow primer directly and liberally to the lower lid.

B. Blend swiftly and evenly from lash line to eyebrow using a laydown brush.

C. Ensure there are no missed spots and that it is seamlessly blended.

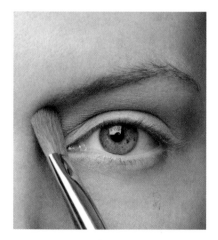

D. Sweep into the inner corner of the eye.

Eye Color and Lash Enhancement

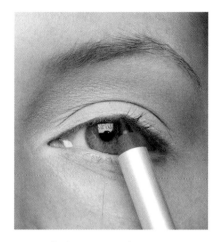

A. Look down into the mirror with your chin up. Dot a gel pencil at the base of the lashes, not on the waterline.

B. See how this technique creates the look of a naturally full lash line.

C. For a natural look, use the tip of your mascara wand and wiggle up through the tips.

D. See how this technique creates softly enhanced lashes.

Triangle of Light

A. Apply under-eye brightener in the shape of a large upside-down triangle under each eye.

B. Extend the triangle down the length of the nose and up the cheekbones.

C. Ensure you are well blended up to the lower lash lines.

D. Gently press into the skin using a cream face brush.

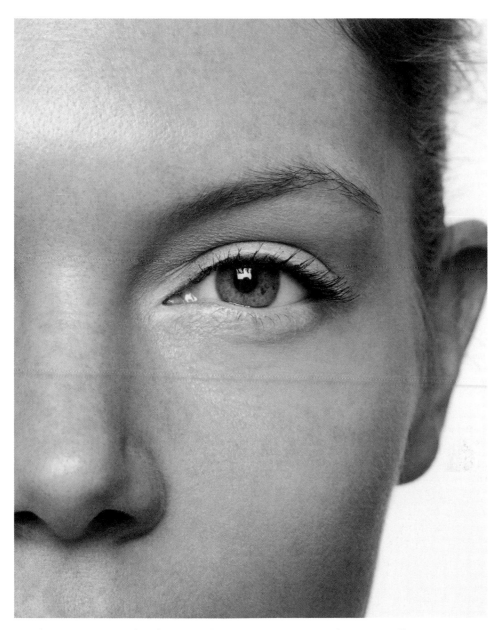

Applying your Triangle of Light before evening out your skin tone will address a range of concerns and enable you to use less foundation.

Even Skin

A. Buff liquid foundation into the skin using a circular motion.

B. Ensure you have accessed small contours using a small domed brush.

C. Apply tinted powder over your foundation for additional coverage.

D. See how evening out the skin's tone enables every feature to stand out.

Face Color and Lip Enhancement

A. Press gel cheek color onto the apples of the cheeks and blend up toward the temple.

B. Press a hydrating, high-shine gloss over the lips.

I love how this nude look brings out Lauren's features without the look of a lot of makeup.

Eye Color and Lash Enhancement

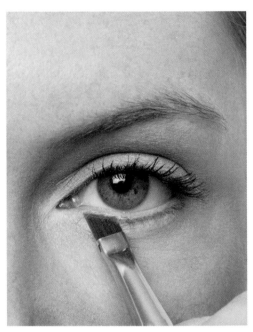

A. Dress up the eyes by pressing a light shimmering shadow onto the center of the lids.

B. Softly define the lower lash lines with a medium-toned shadow and eyelining brush.

C. Brighten the upper brow bone.

D. Brush mascara across the lower lashes.

Even Skin

A. Prior to applying foundation, use a corrector to address areas of concern, such as under-eye hollowness.

B. Press gently for coverage.

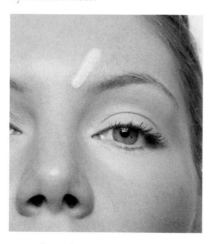

C. Soften furrow lines between brows.

D. Press to blend.

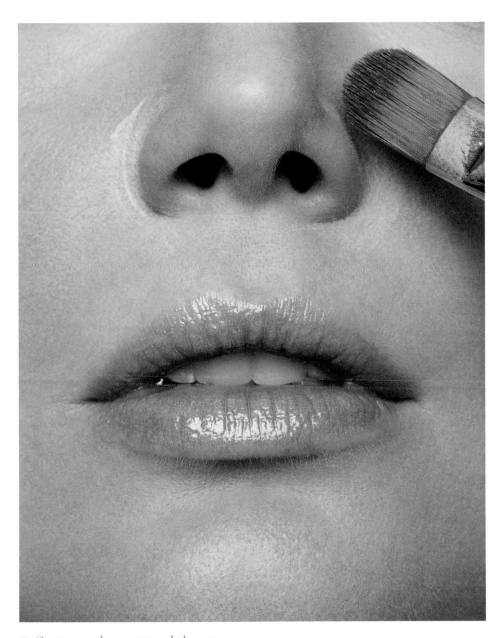

E. Correct redness around the nose.

Brow Enhancement

A. Measure where you want your brow to begin, in line with your nose and the inner corner of your eye.

B. Measure where you want to arch, in line with your nose and pupil.

C. Measure where you want it to end, in line with your nose and the outer corner of your eye.

D. Fill in your brow in short, light strokes.

Lip Enhancement

A. Apply lip color using a lip brush for a soft, yet precise application.

B. Define your lips' shape with lip liner, starting at the Cupid's bow and working down the natural lip line.

Up-leveling

The difference between Lauren's looks are simple but profound.
We filled in her brows then heightened her coloring on the cheeks
and lips for a brighter look that still enhances her natural beauty.

Eye Color

A. Apply a deep-toned shadow across the upper lashes.

B. Blend it slightly upward for a soft, smoky line.

C. Using a liquid pen, line the outer corner of the upper lashes.

D. Highlight the lower waterline with an eye-brightening pencil.

Lash Enhancement

A. Place false lashes along the upper lash line.

B. Gently press them into place using the end of a makeup brush.

C. Use liner to meld your false and natural lashes.

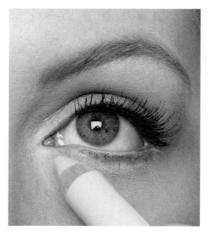

D. Ensure the inner corner is light and bright!

Lip Enhancement

Apply a deep matte lip color.

Maude

All About the Eyes!

A. Apply upper-eye brightener across the lower lid.

B. Blend well.

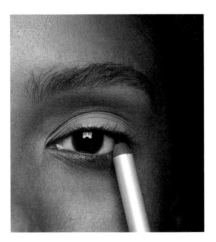

C. Dot a gel pencil between the lashes, not on the waterline.

D. Apply mascara.

Simply brightening and defining Maude's eyes give
her the perfect everyday eye look.

Triangle of Light

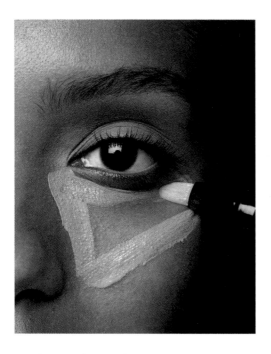

A. Place under-eye brightener
in an upside-down triangle.

B. Distribute evenly over the area
and press gently until blended.

See how this step not only brightens darkness but lifts the face.

Even Skin

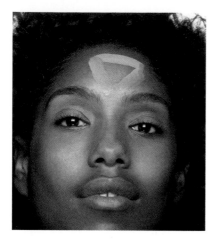

A. To brighten the center of the face, place a lighter foundation in an upside-down triangle in the center of the forehead.

B. Press gently until blended.

C. Place the lighter foundation around the mouth.

D. Press gently until blended.

E. Place foundation that matches your skin tone near the hairline.

F. Press it into the skin to achieve a seamless look.

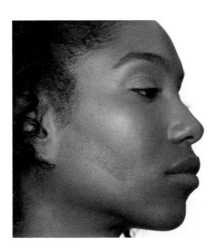

G. Apply under the cheekbone.

H. Set and perfect with translucent powder using a fan brush.

Face Color

Apply a pop of blush to the apples of the cheeks.

Brow Enhancement

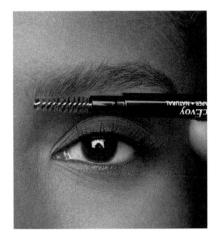

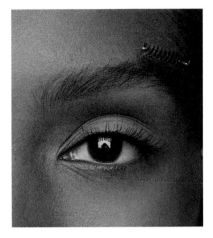

A. Brush the brows into place…

B. …from the start to the end of the brow.

C. Work brow mascara through the brows…

D. …to build onto your natural brow.

Lip Enhancement

Apply a luminous light lip color.

Eye Color

A. Liberally apply a light shimmering shadow across the lower lid.

B. Define the outer corner of the eye.

C. Bring definer down the lower lash line.

D. Connect the two lines at the outer corner of the eye.

Brow Enhancement

A. Fill in sparseness with a precise brow pencil.

B. Define the outline of the brow.

C. Blend color through the brows.

D. Ensure they are brushed into place.

Lip Enhancement

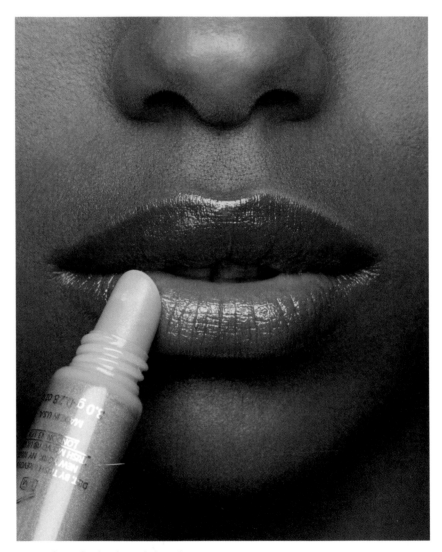

Complete the look with lip gloss

Eye Color

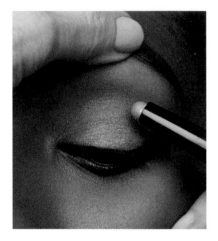

A. Apply a cream shimmer shadow to the center of the eyelid.

B. Blend up to the crease using a small, densely packed brush.

C. Blend across the lower lid.

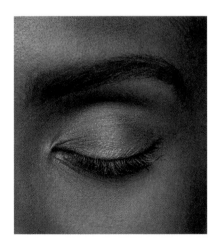

D. See how the shimmer texture brings out the eyelid's dimension.

E. Sweep a light shimmer shadow underneath the arch of the brow.

F. Blend out across the brow bone to accentuate its shape.

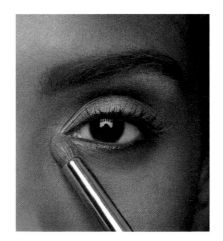

G. Dust the inner corner of the eye.

H. See how this step widens and brightens the eye.

Lash Enhancement

A. Go for it! False lash application can be easy: Apply a thin line of colorless glue to the lash band and set along the upper lashes.

B. Gently press into place for 10 seconds to let dry.

C. Subtle false lashes can dramatically enhance the shape of the eye without an overdone look.

D. Apply a smoky eye color in the crease of the eye to complete a dramatic eye.

Face Color and Lip Enhancement

A. Apply highlight to the high points of the face.

B. See how this technique shapes the face with light.

C. Apply nude lip color, which is always the perfect compliment to a smokey eye.

D. Finish with a sheer gloss.

Donna

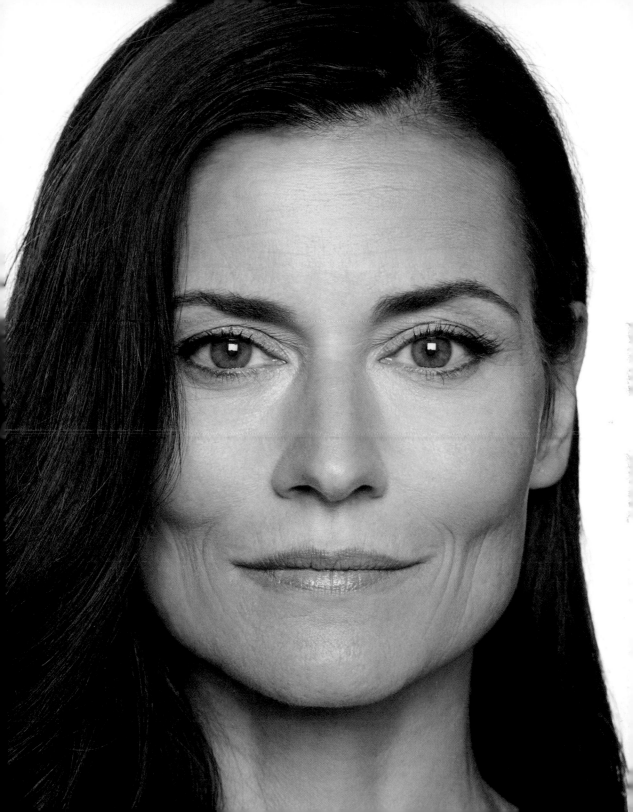

Prep and Prime

Donna exfoliates every day to address the cell turnover
that slows with age. This helps her diminish the appearance
of lines and ensure her complexion looks bright.

A. Apply upper-eye brightener liberally and blend swiftly.

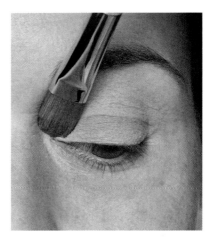

B. Do not miss the inner corner of the eye.

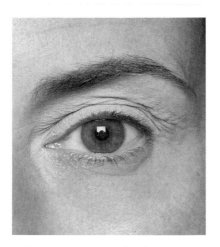

C. Ensure it is seamlessly blended—no bare patches!

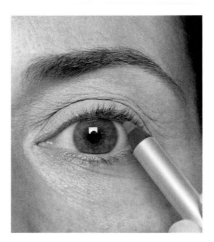

D. Dot a gel liner pencil between the lashes for the look of a naturally defined eye.

Lash Enhancement

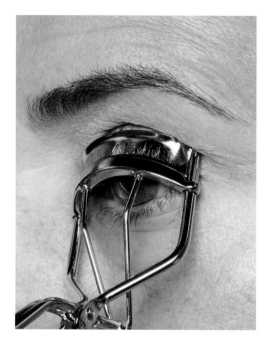 

A. If you are curler shy, give it a chance! The results are worth it: a wider-open eye, a clean lash line ready for makeup, a natural look. Press and hold for 10 seconds.

B. See how beautifully mascara applies to pre-curled lashes.

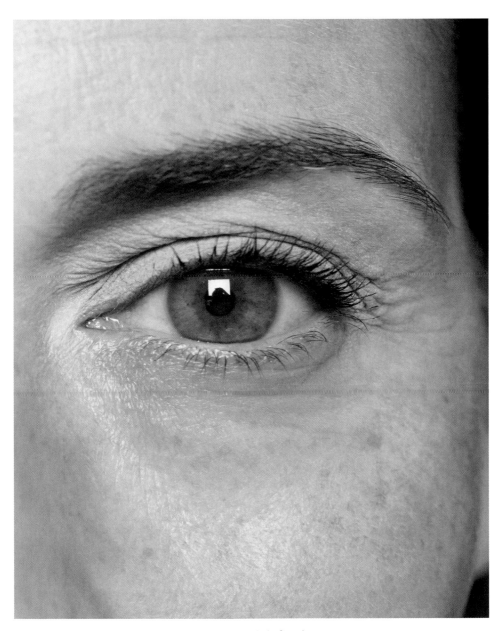

A little can go a long way. A brightened and defined eye
was all Donna needed to refresh her look.

Triangle of Light

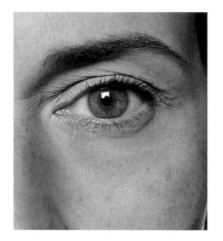

A. Send bags packing!

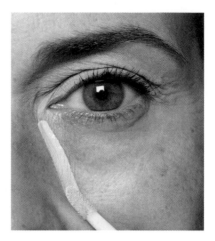

B. Apply under-eye brightener in the Triangle of Light.

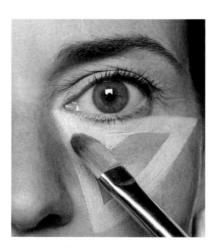

C. Fill in the triangle.

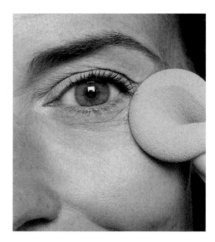

D. Press into the skin with a sponge for the most coverage.

Adding light to the center of the face will give you the lift you are looking for.

Even Skin

A. Stipple foundation into the skin using a flat-topped nylon brush.

B. Press into the skin using a sponge for a full-coverage yet skin-like finish.

The right foundation makes you look like yourself, only better.

Face Color

A. For the most natural-looking warmth, use a deeper shade of foundation as your bronzer to define your facial structure.

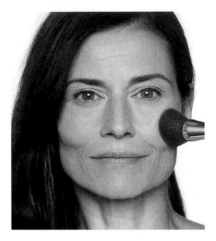

B. Apply it in a 3-shape, starting from the hairline to the cheek.

C. Bring it around the jawline to complete the 3.

D. Blend it onto the neck.

See how this technique gives Donna the look of an instant vacation.

Lip Enhancement

A tint of pink is my go-to for an instant pick-me-up.

Donna is naturally regal with just her skin tone
evened out and her color popped up.

Eye Color and Lash Enhancement

A. Apply a light shimmer cream shadow across the upper lash line.

B. Bring it across the lower lash line.

 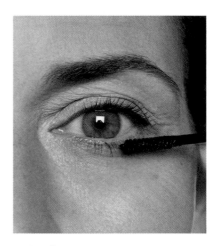

C. Use a liquid liner just at the outer corner of the eye.

D. Apply mascara to the lower lashes.

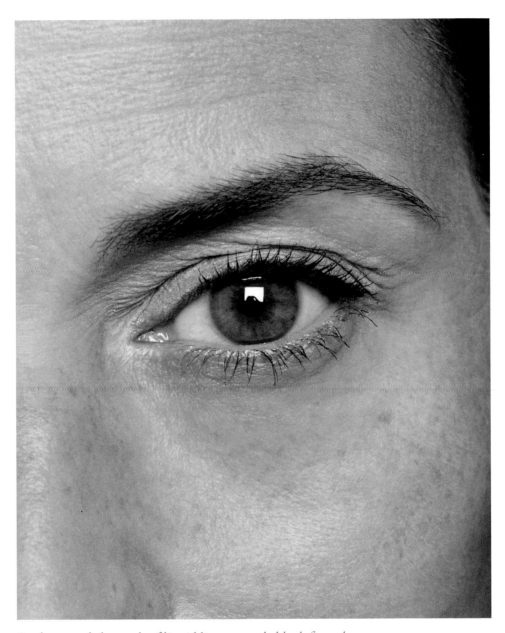

See how a subtle touch of liquid liner remarkably defines the eye.

Triangle of Light

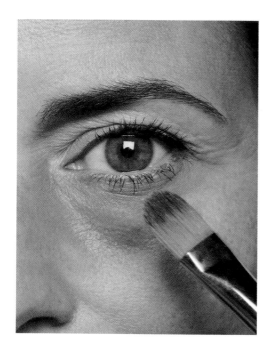

A. Apply an orange-based corrector if you have extreme darkness.

B. Follow with the Triangle of Light.

Even Skin and Face Color

A. Apply foundation.

B. Use a small brush to capture the details.

C. Apply cream cheek color.

Brow Enhancement

Brush brow mascara through the brows
in the direction of hair growth.

Lip Enhancement

A. Apply a deep lip color.

B. Use a lip brush for a precision application whenever you use deep lip color.

Eye Color

A. Press a white eye shadow onto the brow bone.

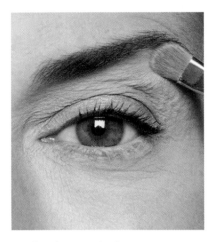

B. Blend up to the brow.

C. Apply powder eye definer to the outer corner of the upper lash line and flick it slightly up using an eyelining brush.

D. Softly define the outer corner of the lower lash line with the color that remains on the brush.

The secret's in the angle. A well-placed flick can make all the difference in the world. Make sure yours is aimed at the temple, or a 45-degree angle from the outer corner of the eye.

Lash Enhancement

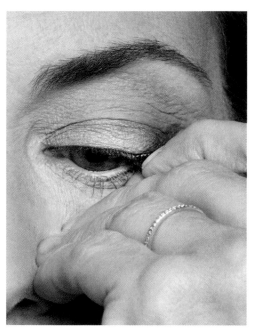

A. Place a half strip of false lashes (sometimes called a demi) at the outer corner of the eye.

B. See how this step elongates the shape of the eye and gives the lift right where you want it.

True or False: Those are Donna's lashes? It'll be our little secret.

Lip Enhancement

Finish with lip color. Light or deep, the key is in the precision.

Donna's Level 3 look is a perfect example of how the Levels of Beauty reflect time spent and attention to detail—not just more obvious makeup.

Alle

Brighten and Prime the Upper Eye

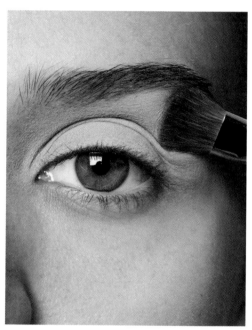

A. Apply brightening shadow primer directly and liberally to the lower lid.

B. Blend swiftly and evenly from the lash line to the eyebrow using a laydown brush.

Eye Color and Lash Enhancement

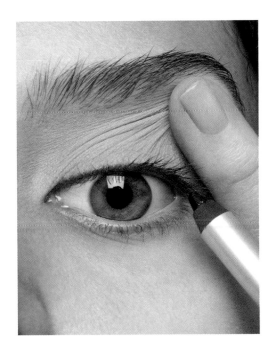

A. Dot a gel liner pencil between the lashes.

B. Apply curling mascara.

Triangle of Light

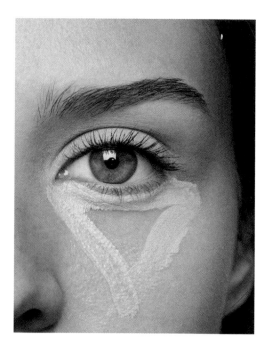

A. Apply under-eye brightener in an upside-down triangle under each eye.

B. Press into the skin until blended.

Even on Alle's bright, unlined eye, this step still enhances her look.

Even Skin

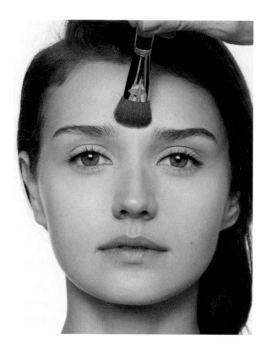 

Apply a sheer layer of foundation only where coverage is needed.
A good formula will undetectably blend right into your skin.

Face Color

Apply a wash of bronzer in a 3-shape, from hairline to
cheekbone to jawline, at the sides of the face.

Face Color

Sweep a veil of blush over the apples of the cheeks.

Eye Color

A. Apply a medium-toned shadow into the crease of the eye.

B. Stroke a cream or powder eye brightener to the brow bone.

C. Place eye brightener onto the inner corner of the eye.

D. Blend with your ring finger.

E. Dab a light bright shadow onto the inner corner of the eye using a precise shadow brush.

F. Dust it along the lower lash line.

Lip Enhancement

A. Apply a deep lip color using a lip brush.

B. Line lips for the most natural look.

A. Apply a deep shadow into the crease using a short, densely packed tapered crease brush.

B. Extend the shadow beyond the outer corner of the eye in a V shape.

C. Blend using a face brush for a soft effect.

D. See all the drama, none of the excess.

E. Apply gray eyeliner to the outer corner of the eye.

F. Apply false lashes.

Lash Enhancement

A. Apply black liquid liner across the upper lash line.

B. Apply curling mascara to the upper lashes.

C. Apply a detail mascara along the lower lashes.

Face Color

A. Apply bronzer using a shorter, densely packed brush for deeper pigmentation.

B. Apply from the hairline to along the cheekbone.

Brow Enhancement

A. Comb brow up and out.

B. Brush brow mascara through brow.

C. Fill in sparseness with a precise brow pencil.

D. Don't forget to brighten above the brow.

See how the warm crease color and a full brow unite
to intensify Alle's look in a chic, wearable way.

Lip Enhancement

Complete the look with a bright lip gloss. Blot down with your ring finger.

BEAUTY CONCERNS
AND MAKEUP SOLUTIONS

The questions I am most often asked pertain to women's personal beauty concerns about their skin and facial features. I would love for us all to see ourselves in a more positive light, but the truth is that we tend to perceive our flaws first. The following five models demonstrate the most common issues and show how to easily address them with the **Power of Makeup**.

As a model in both of my books more than ten years apart, Valerie exemplifies the typical adjustments one may make between the ages of twenty and thirty. In this photo from the first book, Valerie had few concerns. Our interest was in simply improving upon nature. A little light eye shadow, tinted moisturizer, and gloss were all she needed to let her beauty shine. Turn the page to see Valerie's concerns ten years later and how we solve them.

Uneven Skin Tone

SOLUTIONS: To address Valerie's uneven skin tone at age thirty for this book, I used a generous amount of upper- and under-eye brighteners and BB cream to correct and enhance. I then restored healthy coloring with bronzer and blush. I also filled in her lash line with gel liner and used mascara and a brow pencil to define her eye area.

Under-Eye Darkness, Symmetry

SOLUTIONS: For under-eye darkness, I applied an orange-based corrector to Amanda's darkest area, right under the lower lash line. Then I generously applied under-eye brightener in the Triangle of Light. I finished with an extra layer of brightener in the hollow indentation under her eyes. Amanda also wanted more symmetrical features. The addition of foundation over her nose and mouth corrected shadowing, which allowed her face to look more balanced. Lip liner helped correct the asymmetry in her lips.

Complexion and Coloring, Thin Lashes and Brows

SOLUTIONS: After smoothing out and warming Selina's skin tone with foundation, I focused on defining her lashes and brows. I lined between her lashes with a gel pencil, traced her upper and lower lash lines with eye definer, applied mascara, and finished with false lashes. I used a brow pencil and brow mascara to fill in sparseness and build onto her natural eyebrows. Most of Selina's makeup time will be spent on defining these features to achieve her most confident look.

Uneven Skin, Lack of Eye Definition

SOLUTIONS: To allow the beauty of Cherie's facial structure to come out, I had to correct her skin tone. I applied under-eye brightener in the Triangle of Light, chose a full-coverage foundation, and then spent time lightening up and lifting her face using bronzer, highlight, and blush. Cherie has petite eyelids, so I relied on liner, mascara, and false lashes to open her eyes with just the right amount of precise definition.

Loss of Firmness and Definition

SOLUTIONS: To rejuvenate Lisa's face, I focused on using corrector under her foundation to lift and brighten expression lines, as well as the nasolabial folds around her mouth. I used bronzer, highlight, and blush to articulate her cheek structure, which made a tremendous difference. False lashes, a brow pencil, and brow mascara were the keys to correcting her thin lashes and over-plucked eyebrows.

Drooping Eyelids,
Loss of Lip Volume

SOLUTIONS: Chris has gorgeous full cheeks, but she has lost elasticity around her eyes and volume in her lips. Upper-eye brightener brought back her lids, while liner and mascara gave her long but colorless lashes a dramatic lift. Lip liner redefined her lips, while a lip-perfecting balm and light-reflective gloss filled in crinkles and created the illusion of fuller lips.

Facing The Future

HOW TO NAVIGATE THE ROAD AHEAD

T

he question you're now facing, is this: What will it take for you to keep up this new routine? How can you maintain this new sense of self, this new image and perspective, this *new you*? The moment you chose to read this book with the intention of making a change, you took the first step. If you have read this far, you know what you need to do going forward. Let me remind you:

The soul of confidence begins with gifting yourself the time to put your best face forward.

Will you ever fall off the wagon and for days, weeks, maybe months "let yourself go" while out of the beauty routine? We're all human, so yes you might expect that. But then ask yourself: When did you decide to stop? *Why?* Try to get back in the game quickly. Recommit. Find your motivators. Be a believer, not a skeptic. Look at those selfies. Stay mindful of your needs and the big results you can get so quickly with such simplicity. Do not get comfortable again with old habits and complacency. Remember how important investing in you can be. Your future and present self will thank you. This is about agelessness.

Consistency is paramount. Humans are creatures of habit. Women, especially, are anchors in life's patterns that make the world go around. The body—and brain—love consistency. In medical terms, doctors call it homeostasis. I call it harmony. And it's achieved easily through the simple Gift of Time to put myself together in the morning in a way that brings out my very best. I can then harmonize what's going on in my life effortlessly and easily. It infuses me with joy and confidence, and then I carry that out into the world for others to see and enjoy. I bring harmony first to myself, then share it with others.

Not every day needs to be exactly the same, and it won't. Of course there will be days when you look great and days you won't. My hope for you is that 99 percent of the time, you look in the mirror and love what you see—no matter what. And you will maintain a semblance of uniformity by creating and sustaining a certain pattern to your days. You will build new habits that will keep you on track and living up to the principles of beauty confidence. Self-care should not be an on-and-off proposition. This is true whether we're talking about a makeup routine or how you eat or exercise. Finding your own unique version of consistency across all the ways that support your personal self-care will be key to your success.

ENJOY THE GIFT OF BEAUTY

Makeup isn't everything in this world. Your beauty is not your greatest purpose, and your reason for living is not to put makeup on. But let me tell you this: If you harness the power of the Beauty Cascade, you will live with greater confidence, joy, and purpose. You will get more of what you want. You will find daily challenges easier to deal with. And you will find fulfillment easier to come by in all you do. I can promise you that. When you put your time and passion into what allows you to exude the best of all of you, you win. Consider that your ultimate mission in life. Give yourself permission to do just that.

TRISH'S TOP PRINCIPLES TO LIVE BY

These are my nonnegotiables—the ways I aim to think and act so that I do my best every single day no matter what life throws at me. Highlight the ones that resonate with you. Come up with a few of your own. Create a pretty document of your personal collection of principles that you can post in your bathroom (perhaps next to that "after" selfie). Visit them every day. Remind yourself of who you are, and what you want to be:

- Accept who you are and make the most of what you have.
- Surround yourself with people who bring you up—not down. Don't get sucked into other people's chaos.
- Don't dwell on the negative. It gets you nowhere.
- Think not of yesterday, but of today and tomorrow.
- Organize your time. Don't waste it.
- Do the work. Don't procrastinate. Be appreciative, straightforward, generous, and gracious.
- Don't apologize for the way you look.
- Take responsibility for your actions and choices— you are in charge of YOU—and give yourself credit for your accomplishments.
- Count your blessings, love yourself, and be grateful for what you have.
- Enjoy the present; it is a gift.
- Start your day with: *Who do I choose to be today?*

SHOW UP IN EVERY SINGLE MOMENT LIKE YOU'RE MEANT TO BE THERE.

–Marie Forleo

WHO ARE YOU TODAY?

Who do I choose to be today? This question is critical because here's the thing: Every single day—every single minute, in fact—you change. I mean that from a purely physical—biological—standpoint, as well as figuratively. Physically, we know that the body is constantly undergoing adaptations depending on the kind of environment we're in and lifestyle influences. In the last decade, scientists have discovered that our biology is determined more by how our DNA behaves than by the actual genes we inherit. We have the power to switch our genes on and off based on environmental cues—what we eat, the exercise we do, the surroundings we live in, the tasks we spend our time doing, the interactions we have, and so on. This, in turn, influences our physiology, our features, and our overall health and well-being. Your body will not be the same ten years from now, and neither is it the same as ten years ago. And this is a good thing, especially when we take the time to care for it every step of the way.

Figuratively, you know that you evolve over time from a macro view. How you think and feel is different today than just last year (and probably yesterday, too!). Your responsibilities, your time constraints, your daily schedule, your habits and routines, your moods and way of thinking, and even your relationship with makeup and sense of confidence shift as you course through life. Sometimes these shifts happen rather suddenly, as with marriage, a new job, the birth of children, a diagnosis, or the death of a loved one. At other times, they occur gradually and rather subtly. You may not have made a conscious effort to change your hair and clothing styles, but if you were to look at a photograph of yourself from fifteen or twenty years ago, you'd notice a difference. The changes happened naturally, and genuinely.

The Beauty Cascade of a single twenty-something won't be identical to a married woman in her forties or a retiree in her seventies. Your Beauty Cascade will evolve with you as your needs, your lifestyle, your state of mind, and your tastes and preferences spontaneously move. The goal is to be open to changes over time. Navigate and modify your Beauty

Cascade as you do with your general life: Find the motivation to keep it going day after day, year after year, despite experiences that try to derail you or change you on the spot. Even your motivators and incentives will vary in disparate stages of your life. Stop and identify new ones when the old ones aren't working anymore. This is what makes life so wonderful—it's constantly in motion, it's fluid, it compels us to keep going, and we get to choose how to travel through it and negotiate our choices as they emerge. Stay fearless, brave, and seek new adventures. Give yourself the Gift of Time whenever you can. Tweak your Beauty Cascade as needed along the way. Face your future with excitement and resolve. Life is a matter of focus, and it can be filled with beauty if you so choose.

Come back to this book when you feel that your routine needs an upgrade or refresher course. Milestone events or birthdays can be good check-in points. Take an extra five minutes in front of the mirror when you hit an important moment or stage in your life. Be proud that you've gotten to where you are and think about where you'd like to go from here. Harness that connection between looking your best and feeling your best, knowing that you can always work *from the outside in*. You can hit the reboot button whenever you like. This is true whether we're talking about the nuts and bolts of a proper makeup application attuned to your current Level and style, or just finding time for yourself and your self-care. Stay attuned to your needs as you metamorphose throughout your life.

Never forget: Every day presents an opportunity to put your best face—your best self—forward. You can choose to have boundless confidence at every age. And it can begin with that single question: *Who do I choose to be today?* Take ownership of your beauty and your life. In the words of Eleanor Roosevelt, one of the most confident, storied women in history, "Life is what you make it. Always has been, always will be."

Confident women are the ones you want to be around because they emit a certain gravitational force. **Style, elegance, and poise reflect a universal language.** It's a language that goes far beyond the tangible things in life. It's the way we move in our space, the way we smile, the way we carry ourselves, the look in our eyes, the posture we maintain, the confidence we exhibit, the way we live our lives and communicate with others. It's a language that holds a lot of power—power that connects us all and instills in us a magnificently strong sense of individual self.

PRODUCT INDEX

Under-Eye Brightener
Water-Based Foundation
Medium Bronzer
Shimmering Pink Blush
Precise Brow Pencil
Sheer Pink Lip Color

SELINA

PAGE 189

Eye Shadow Primer in Brightening Shade
Gel Liner in Black
Eggshell Eye Shadow
Powdered Eyeliner
Tubular Volumizing Mascara
False Lashes with Clear Band
Under-Eye Brightener
Water-Based Foundation
Translucent Powder
Matte Bronzer
Cream Blush
Precise Brow Pencil
Fiber Brow Mascara
Pink Conditioning Lip Balm

CHERIE

PAGE 191

Eye Primer in Brightening Shade
Gel Liner in Black
Cream Eye Shadow
Kohl Eyeliner in Taupe
Tubular Curling Mascara
False Lashes with Clear Band
Under-Eye Brightener
Full Coverage Foundation
Translucent Powder
Champagne Highlight

Medium Bronzer
Soft Pink Blush
Precise Brow Pencil
Sheer Pink Gloss

LISA

PAGE 193

Eye Shadow Primer in Brightening Shade
Gel Liner in Aubergine Tone
Long-Wear Eye Shadow Pen
  in Shimmering Golden Bronze
Eye Brightening Pencil
Tubular Curling Mascara
False Lashes with Clear Band
Water-Based Foundation
Champagne and Bronze Highlight
Gel Blush
Precise Brow Pencil
Soft Pink Lip Color
Rose-Toned Lip Color
Lip Liner in Medium Nude Tone
Vibrant Pink Lipstick

CHRIS

PAGE 195

Eye Primer in Brightening Shade
Gel Liner in Black
Tubular Curling Mascara
Under-Eye Brightener
BB Cream
Translucent Powder
Medium Bronzer
Sheer Blush
Lip Liner in Nude Tone
Pink Conditioning Lip Balm
Light Reflective Gloss

ACKNOWLEDGMENTS

As the saying goes, "It takes a village…" and I have the best village in the world. Here are a few words on those who have been integral in bringing this book to life:

First and foremost, thank you to my legendary agent and friend, Jill Cohen, who made this book happen. Jill, you have been my voice of reason. My confidante and confidence instiller. You are a bottomless well of kindness and a model of industriousness, judgment, ideas, and self-control. I will be forever thankful for the many months of hearing me out, keeping me on track, trusting my gut while giving me yours, and being willing to change any course at any hour when that's what it took to get it right. Your energy and optimism are in a class of their own and sustained me throughout this emotional, challenging, and ultimately beautiful process.

Thank you to my editor, Karen Rinaldi, and the team at Harper Wave for believing this was more than a tutorial. Thank you to my magical coauthor, the one and only Kristin Loberg, for giving this project the best of yourself in spite of the personal heartbreak you have endured this year. You brought the science, gift, and power of my ideas to life and shaped this story as only you could have.

A special thank-you to Lizzie Cohen whose mark is on every word and picture in this book, to say nothing of its actual existence. Your book publishing savvy, tireless partnership, pursuit of excellence, insane work ethic, and support as a bridge between me and every hand in this project are what kept it together and brought it to the finish line. It would not have happened without you. Thank you to my voice and communications director, Cassandra Csencsitz, for your depth and attention to our storytelling over the past ten years. I couldn't have asked for a more brilliant writer.

To my designer, Doug Turshen, I was an admirer of yours long before I knew the man behind the art or that one day you would grace my own book. And grace it you did, handling my challenges and changes with patience and poise like no other. I have the highest respect for your talent and eye and the deepest gratitude for the calm and understanding behind them. Thank you to you and Steve Turner for your beautiful work. You have been my dream team.

To my amazing photography team: Ondrea Barbe, you make makeup shine. Your exquisite eye for detail allow each pigment and stroke to jump off the page. Antonis Achilleos, your still lifes are larger than life. Greg Delves, I'm so pleased to have your beautiful portraits included, too. Alexa Mulvihill and Shana Faust, I so enjoyed our collaboration on the cover.

I thank the beautiful faces that fill these pages. Models are the epitome of strength and vulnerability, urgency and patience. You work harder than anyone could ever know. Thank you for all the washing and posing and expressions of self. A special thank-you to Valerie for her repeat performance; it was beautiful to work with you again.

Thank you to Tamara Dominguez and Richard Grandinetti, the lead makeup artists who gave their beautiful talent to this book. Tamara, my friend, you are always there when I need you and represent me to perfection when I am not. Richard, it has been such a joy sharing this entire journey with you. Thank you for being beside me at the beginning and the perfect ambassador for our brand ever since. Also, a special thank-you to Rosa Barney, Larry Baquerizo, Rosie Manousos, and Dru McDaniel all of whom contributed to the makeup. And where would makeup be without hair? Thank you to my incomparable Katie Schember; L'Appartement owner, Tiffany Kaljic, who is there for my team's and my hair no matter the hour; and the wonderful stylist Micaela Vera whom I respect so much. Together they coiffed our models flawlessly and kept every hair in place throughout every shoot.

To my Trish family, I love going to work and coming home each day because of you. Thank you to my wonderful personal teams in New York and Southampton for your endless acts of kindness and care toward me and Ron, in sickness and in health, over so many miles and years. To my New York and New Jersey marketing and sales teams, thank you for giving me the best of yourselves, doing amazing work, and making it so much fun. Our shared creativity and collaboration is the greatest satisfaction in my life. To my sales team leaders and artists around the country and world, you are my pride and joy. Each day you hold my message and our clients' faces in your hands. Thank you for being the connecting point between our brand and the women who what we do is all about. I see and appreciate each and every one of you.

Last but not least, thank you to all the women who have sat in my chair, at once receiving and inspiring the Power of Makeup in a give-and-take that has been the greatest joy of my career. I have grown through my quest to meet your needs while our conversations—on beauty and so much more—have never ceased fueling my mind and touching my heart. This is a book that transcends makeup. It is about making the choices that are right for you. It is for and about *you*.

CREDITS

PHOTOGRAPHERS

All photographs by Ondrea Barbe except:

Cover by Alexa Mulvihill and Shana Faust

Pages v, 6, 12, 20, 36–39, 46, 52, 62–63, 196 by Antonis Achilleos

Page 183 by Danielle Frederici

Pages 190–191, 205 by Giles Hooper

Pages vi middle left, 61 lower left, 184-189, 194-195 by Greg Delves

PROP STYLIST

Pages 6, 12, 20, 46, 52, 62–63, 196 by Elizabeth Press

MODELS

Alle Johnson, Amanda Salvato, Andjela Milanovic, Atikah Karim, Cherie Mendez, Chris Stewart, Donna Rothballer, Kseniya Baranaua, Lauren Walshe, Lisa Masters, Maude Bourek, Sam Gold, Selina White, Valerie Aydeyeva

CASTING AGENTS

Jan Planit, Steve Willis